Imagine All
the Flossibilities!
Jackie Salveson

CURIOUS WORLD

of Dandy-Lion

Written by Lorraine Hawley
Illustrated by Jocie Salveson

LAWLEY
PUBLISHING

Dedicated to my Dandelion friends—those distracted by flickering lights, shuffling papers, smelly gym socks, itchy clothes, foods that should never touch, and textures too yuck to consume. And to their parents and teachers who strive to understand.

—LH

For Craig, Caden, Cody and Kylie. I love you more than you can imagine.

—JS

TABLE OF CONTENTS

1

Jinxed

Tiny beetle feet scamper across my bedroom desk and tickle my arm.

Kssch! Kssch! Floss hisses. His shiny black armor twitches and two beady eyes stare at me.

"Not today, Floss. You can't be here. This day is too important." I wrap my arm around my journal to block his view. Attention steady on my checklist, I hover the pen over the first box, *Ignore Floss.*

Floss scuttles over and nudges my hand with his swirly-q nose horn. Bump. My pen strays.

"I know you want to help, but you can't. You're not real," I tell the rhinoceros beetle.

He wobbles back, then lumbers forward. This time, his pointed head horn aims my way.

Bump. *Kssch!* I suppress a laugh and put down the pen. It's not Floss's fault that he doesn't know the stakes today. I have to make a friend who will help me. I've tried everything else. I can't break the jinx on Mr. Dally by myself.

"Meredith, you'd better hurry, or you'll be late!" Mom shouts from downstairs. "And don't forget to brush your hair."

I slam the journal shut and turn to Floss. "Fine. You can stay. But no matter what, don't show up at school. Got it?" I tip my pinky to him.

Floss rubs his beetle wings in a refusal to promise. *Poof.* He disappears.

"Be right there!" I tromp across the wood floor to get my hairbrush. The attic overhead groans, cracking its old bones. Grams swears our house has arthritis. A quick brush to get the knots out changes nothing. My hair's whitish-blonde and cotton ball wispy. Most of the time, it looks like I stuck my finger in an electric socket.

Time's up. I tuck the journal into my backpack and toss the bag over my shoulder, taking two stairs at a time.

Mom rushes from the kitchen to meet me at the stair landing. "Don't forget your lunch." She shoves a brown paper bag into my hands.

"Did you pack—"

"Ketchup. Yes. Four packets."

"Fine. Thanks," I say, but it's not. I carefully slide the bag into the outside backpack pocket.

"Honey, are you sure you don't want me to walk you to the bus stop?"

"Mom. I'm in fifth grade now." I bolt for the front door before she insists.

When I hit the porch, I pull my shoulders back and hike up my backpack, taking a deep sniff to test the air. Damp cement covered in rotten leaves with a hint of fresh corn.

Today smells like a good day to find a friend.

The bus driver yanks the lever, and the door glides open.

"All aboard!" Mr. Jennings hollers.

Relief washes over me. I know Mr. Jennings. He drove the bus for fourth grade, too. I climb the steps and slide to a window seat near the front, leaving room on the bench beside me. Kids scramble past me and pile into the back.

The bus pulls away, and we pass the Dally's house. The jinx. It's pin-drop quiet. All eyes forward for one, two, three seconds. No one makes a peep—it's not worth the risk.

Finally, we're on the other side. Everyone talks at once. I glance back at the Dally's house and whisper, "I'm trying—promise."

Mr. Dally's wife used to live there with him. Now, he stays there alone. I miss helping in his garden, and I know I should visit, but I can't. Nope. Not until I break the jinx that keeps him trapped in the house.

Conversation ripples. All I can hear is buzzing as if a swarm of flies climbed into my ear. Except the flies are underwater and drowning. The noises are too much, so I cover my ears and hum quietly to myself.

In Mr. Jennings's rearview mirror, I spot a beetle racing seat to seat, checking over the kids. *Oh, Floss.* I almost missed him. Real-kid smells mask his sugary scent. For some reason, all Fancies—that's what I named them because they're shinier than

3

us—smell like they live at an amusement park surrounded by candied apples, deep-fried donuts, and hot chocolate.

I ignore Floss—I don't need any kids making fun of me. But pretending someone's not there when they are, well, it's hard. Floss isn't the first someone I've tried to forget. There was another Fancy, Juniper, a talking-boy ladybug. Then a rainbow-feathered bird named . . . Huh? See, I can't remember.

Doesn't matter. Turns out, I was the only one who could see them.

I flop back in my seat.

Mom said I'd never make real friends if I kept ignoring kids my age to play with Fancies. So, I stopped paying them attention. Nothing changed, though; kids still ignore me. It's better, anyway. Everything I like too much disappears—except for Floss. That beetle's too stubborn to leave me alone. But I don't tell anyone he's around. No one understands, anyway. I'm the only one who can see the other side of real.

To distract my attention away from Floss, I count seat rows. Fifteen on each side. I recognize a few kids from last year. They high-five and huddle together, talking about their summers. It's okay. My new friend and I will high-five and catch up when we meet.

I go over the next item on my checklist: Be friendlier. I glance at my shirt. Printed on the front is a backstroke-swimming gopher and says, *Gopher it*. I wore it on purpose.

"Gopher it. Gopher it," I repeat, a little too loud.

The next row back, some girl yells, "What?"

Oh, she could be my new friend. I turn around to face her. "It's my shirt. I'm telling myself—"

She glares at me and pivots sideways, whispering to the girl beside her.

My face burns red hot, and I slink down in the seat. I wish I never gave up turning invisible.

At the next stop, I scoot closer to the window and chance eye contact with the kids boarding the bus.

Dr. Richter always says, "Making eye contact means you're open for conversation, which is helpful when trying to make friends." Personally, I think it makes you look like a stalker, like the one I watched on late night television before Dad changed the channel. But I force myself to stare at each kid who rushes past me.

Billy Simpson is the last to push his way up the stairs right before the bus doors close. *No way!* I shove my backpack across the bench and shut my eyes tight. Part of me had hoped he moved away over the summer.

Nope. I duck lower and cross my arms to hide the shirt. No way I'm gopher-ing him. The plan is to find a real friend who won't rat me out, not the Billy-type of friend.

The feeling that he's staring at me makes me peek to see what he's doing.

He's standing in front of me, smirking at my backpack. "Look who's here. Mere-a-ditz. I thought they were sending you to a special school this year."

My lips stay zipped.

"Well?"

Everyone stares at me because of Billy's big loud voice. I pull my foot up on the bench seat and double knot my shoe. It's best to ignore him. Mom says encouraging bullies makes them worse.

"Sit down, Mr. Simpson," Mr. Jennings scolds from the driver's seat.

"I'm goin'. I'm goin'." Billy struts past me and high-fives kids like he's king of the bus.

Floss jumps and perches on Billy's head. The beetle marches around his scalp, spurred feet pulling short red hair and forcing strands to stick straight up like horns. Billy scratches his head, but Floss avoids his fingers.

My lip twists. Quickly, I cover my mouth and count road bumps until we pull up at school. Across the schoolyard is a three-story, red-brick building. Students are everywhere. My body tightens, and I can't catch my breath.

Floss leaps onto the bench next to me and wiggles his antennae. *Kssch!*

"Fine. I'll go. But you stay here," I whisper and waggle my finger at him.

Grabbing my stuff, I jump off the bus and find an empty spot by the oak tree. I take out the school map and pretend I'm reading, even though I already know the school's layout—Elmore has forty-two rooms, including a gym, a computer lab, and a cafeteria.

I peek over the map edge. Most kids gather in different circles; a few I know, like Isabel Herrera. She has a blue headband tucked in her brown, curly hair. Alexa Keough's standing beside her, wearing a matching headband in her yellow-blonde hair. They match a lot, except that Isabel's nice and Alexa is not. Last year, when a fire truck drove past our school with sirens blaring, I couldn't help but hide under the desk and cover my ears. Alexa laughed and called me a mutt, saying only dogs hide from sirens.

When I told Grams, she said, "You're a dandelion in a field of clovers. You just be you, and don't pay attention to those mean kids."

That's the truth. I need a friend like Isabel.

She was my almost-best-friend back in second grade. She even invited me to her birthday party. At first, Mom got excited, but I didn't go. Everyone else's envelope had stickers inside, and Isabel signed the "I" in her name with a red glitter heart. When I asked Mom why mine was written in neat cursive without stickers or hearts, she sighed and said it was best I didn't go.

The warning bell rings, and I slam my palms over my ears, counting three short blasts. School starts in five minutes. I drop the map inside the backpack and reach for the journal, sliding my finger down the bookmark to open the first page. Slipping the pen from the spiral holder, I check off number five, *Learn from watching others.* Dr. Richter helped come up with that idea.

When I'm done, I tuck it back into the bag.

Ouch! A sharp poke jabs my finger, a wood sliver sticks from my skin. I pinch the splinter out with my fingernails and press hard to stop the pinprick of blood.

Once it stops, I shuffle through the pack until I find the culprit. My hands clench the popsicle stick frame, and I pull it out, keeping the picture face down and hugging it to my chest. Finding courage, I tip the photo. There, glued to the cardboard, is a picture of me standing between Mr. and Mrs. Dally, holding up a prize-winning zucchini at the Indiana state fair. My grin was so big that my cheeks looked chubby.

That was the day I met the Dallys. I was five years old.

I press my hand to the photo and squeeze my eyes tight. *You can do this.* I concentrate on all twenty-six ideas from my "Make a Friend" checklist. I must be brave to help Mr. Dally.

If I stick to the plan and hide my Fancies, someone will help me break the jinx and save him. I know it.

2

MASHED-POTATO HAIR

The classroom door sits wide open.

Sweat slicks my palms. I pass by kids pushing and yelling and laughing. I inch toward the door, closer and closer. But the doorway sprouts teeth, snarling—the mouth of a lion gapes open, ready to chomp down and shred me to pieces. My sneakers stick to the floor like chewed gum under desks.

The big cat belches thick and greasy; burnt corn dog stench mists the hall.

Holy monkeys! I pinch my nose and wait, watching.

But kids keep moving down the hallway. No one scrunches their nose or dodges the paw swiping at their heads like it's bopping toys.

My fingers twitch, so I reach out a little for the tawny mane almost close enough to touch, yet not. Kids stare and whisper at my outstretched hand, making me feel enormously alone.

The lion's not real. I will my feet to move. It's only Predator Cat hanging around the classroom's entrance. He's one of my

Fancies. I can tell, and not because he's shiny. No one else notices the burping snaggle-tooth taking up half the door.

The final bell rings. It's now or never. I cover my head with my hands and duck through the doorway, exiting safely on the other side.

My moment of relief slips when I scan the room. Now, I wish a lion really would drag me away. Almost everyone has taken a seat except Billy. He's leaning against the edge of his desk, flicking a paper football at the back of a kid's head.

My assigned seat's in the front row, so I have to walk in front of other kids. I squint to make everything teeny and blurry, and now the kids seem far away. I take giant steps and slide into my seat.

The teacher writes her name on the whiteboard: *Ms. Reeder.* At least I'm in the right room. Now, all I need is a nice, boring day—one without Fancies.

Ms. Reeder turns to the class and smiles. She doesn't even look like a teacher. A tulip, maybe. I like flowers. I had a Fancy friend once, Annabelle. She was a daffodil.

"Welcome to fifth grade, everyone. Get ready to have your best year ever."

When the lunch bell dings, I make my way to the cafeteria. The hallways are wide enough, but kids still stop in front of me and talk to their friends. I weave around them and play a game. They're alligators, and I'm trudging through a swamp. Extra points if I don't draw their attention.

Once I get to the cafeteria, I scope out the room. On one side is the hot lunch line and on the other is a make-it-yourself salad bar.

A kid leans under the sneeze guard to scoop croutons on his plate and sneezes in the lettuce. *Disgusting!* I wouldn't eat from a salad bar anyway, and not because of germs. Some are good for you. The human body contains over 100 trillion bacteria cells, which is about ten times more than human cells. Germs are normal. Snot on lettuce is not.

And that's why I bring lunch.

I head to the vending machine—where packaging protects the snacks—and stick in two quarters. After pressing the button for grape juice, the machine shudders, but nothing comes out. Then I see him. Behind the glass, Floss straddles between two boxes, hooking my grape juice with his horns and struggling with all his might to hold back the carton.

"Hey!" I smack the vending machine. "Get out!"

Floss's six chitin legs flail, and his grip slips. He falls to the next slot and the next, knocking the wrong juice box down into the dispenser. My grape juice ignores me from the top shelf.

"That's not the one I wanted," I scold Floss.

An older boy walks by. "That vending machine always gives the wrong drink."

Maybe it does. But this one's on Floss.

I grab the box from the bottom and inspect the label. *Carrot juice?* I didn't even know vegetables had juice. My jaw clenches, then my shoulders, until my whole body stiffens. The inside of me burns hot like my insides are melting. Screaming is the only thing that cools this kind of heat.

"I wanted juice! Regular juice!"

The cafeteria attendant sprints across the room. "Are you okay?"

"I'm fine." I grind my teeth and glare at Floss.

From an empty slot in the vending machine, Floss blows me fake kisses.

"Meredith, right?" The attendant tries to get my attention. "Do you need a quiet place to sit?"

Like sitting will help my carrot juice problem.

"I don't want to sit somewhere quiet. I want grape juice. I bought it, and it's supposed to be grape. You can't even squeeze carrots." I show her the box. "See? It's not real."

Her gaze darts to another attendant across the cafeteria and back to me. What's she so worried about? It's not her carrot juice.

"Come with me, and we'll talk in the hall." She puts her hand on my back.

"No." I nudge away. "I'm staying here. I'll keep the drink."

"Okay." She smiles. "Please take a seat. And no yelling."

"I won't." But my insides don't feel right anymore. Each step I take makes me nervous, like I'm walking to the edge of the high dive board. *One friend,* I tell myself—*for Mr. Dally*—and scan the crowded tables for a place to sit.

There's a girl with seats open next to her, so I force my feet to move.

A red hair bow sits neatly in her hair; the ribbon trail spirals along her black curls. I wish I had curls. One time, I got my hair to grow past my shoulders, but the strands kept breaking off and left ragged hairs sticking straight up from my head. Now, I keep it short.

The closer I get, the better I can read her silver necklace. *Molly.* Even her name is pretty.

With only a few inches to go, I change course. No way I can sit next to Molly. A gaggle of boys surrounds her.

Groups of geese are called gaggles. Boys in groups are called gangs, I think. They act like a gaggle, though, running around and honking to get her attention. Might as well flap their wings. My ears can't handle all their noise. I veer left.

Two tables over, I scout a boy sitting by himself and head his direction. He wears a black hoodie even though it's not cold inside. A few steps closer, and warmth rushes over me; a hazy memory swirls into my head—a boy ladybug flittering behind juniper bushes.

My hand stretches out to touch the ladybug, but he's too far away. I almost reach him and—

"Go away!" I say and snap my hand back in panic, reminding myself to stick to the plan.

Quick, before I change my mind, I plop into the seat across from him and mentally check off, *Sit with someone at lunch.* Dr. Richter says eating with other kids makes you look confident, so it's on the list.

The kid peers up and grunts. I mean, an actual grunt. I decide his name is "Grunt" and consider grunting back, but then there would be two of us grunting.

Grunt.

Grunt!

Grunt, grunt?

Grunt.

That won't work. I unfold the paper bag and flatten out a napkin to place my peanut butter sandwich on—smooth, not crunchy, thinly layered on white bread with the crusts cut off.

Grunt forks brownish meat with gravy into his mouth and chews. His jaw slows, and his eyes narrow. Then he swallows and breaks off a huge smile. "Wow. It is you! How you been, Dandy?"

I flinch and glance over my shoulder. "Are you talking to me?"

"Who else would I be talking to?"

"Are you real?" The urge to poke his hand is too strong, and—

"Ouch." His face momentarily scrunches before going back to his sopping tray lunch. "Yes. At least, I think so."

Just to be safe, I take a deep sniff—no trace of cotton candy or any other amusement park odors. This boy smells like . . . well, a boy. He's real.

"The name's Jax." He spears another chunk of meat and lifts his fork in a toast.

"Jax?" My nose crinkles. "You mean, like Ajax, the cleaning stuff?"

He pauses with his fork midair. "Sure. I guess. But without the A."

"Alright." I return to preparing lunch, placing my bag

14

of ridged potato chips evenly between the row of four Heinz ketchup packets and my apple.

He eyes my setup. "You want your chips?"

Sharing is on my list. I hand them over. My eyes linger on the empty spot in my line-up.

He tosses the chip bag next to his tray. "You want your sandwich?"

My stomach protests, but I hand it over.

"Hmm, how 'bout your apple?"

Is he going to take all my food? I reach for the apple.

His lip quirks, like he's fighting a smile. "Don't give people things that belong to you, Meredith." My name rolls over his tongue as if he's already eaten the peanut butter. "They'll take advantage." He hands the food back to me.

How does he know my name?

I sniff at him again to make sure I didn't miss anything. Nope. He still smells like a boy. The lunch lady called me Meredith. He probably overheard, that's all.

My attention sticks to the finger-indents he left on my sandwich. The growl in my belly is begging me to ignore them and take a bite. Not a chance. Fingers have the worst germs.

"Goodbye, peanut butter," I whisper at the squished sandwich before wrapping it up in a napkin. I brush my hands together, rip off the ketchup's corners, and squeeze a red mound onto the plastic baggie's corner. Mom used to pack six packets—I need that many to make the best ketchup pile. But the more packets I ask for, the more my parents fight about how many I should take.

Dr. Richter explained that I use ketchup to calm my flavor

palette, but mom says that doesn't mean I should go overboard. I'm what's called "A Supertaster." It isn't as cool as it sounds. Supertasters have more tongue bumps or "papillae," making us sensitive to taste and textures. Add in my super-smelling nose along with my extra-sensitive ears and eyes, and I'm one giant fluffball of receptors.

Jax's finger picks carrots off his tray. "No, thank you."

Nothing about me is regular. To kids at school, I'm that odd girl who still plays pretend, thanks to Floss. To my parents, I'm better known as "The Situation."

Go to your room until your dad and I figure out what to do about the situation, Meredith. I'm that sort of problem, the kind with only two solutions. People either ignore me, or they treat me with an uncomfortable dose of pity.

"And last, the milk." Jax chugs down what's left in his carton and crushes it. He belches and casually grins at me.

What's with this boy?

Head low, I sneak a peek at him and lock on his eyes. They're earthy, like potting soil. No. Like an acorn cap. Mine are brown too, but more like puddles of muddy water after a storm.

On Jax's left wrist is a watch like my dad wears, with an oversized round face and a trio of clock hands. The brown leather strap is cracked. Is that what popular kids are wearing this year? I wonder if my dad will let me borrow his.

I dredge the chips through ketchup and munch while pretending I'm not sneaking sideways glances at him. Then suddenly, something gooey smacks the back of my head; chunks of white splatter across the table and onto Jax. I swipe at my head, and a glob of mashed potato plops into my hand. The rest

16

sticks to my cotton hair.

Jax glances at me, then down at the potato splotches on his black hoodie. He grabs my apple and hurls it over my head. Not a lob, like a NERF ball—he flings it with the arm of an Indiana Hoosier pitcher.

Smack.

I twist around in my seat in time to see Billy Simpson grasp at his bright red ear. The apple rolls away on the floor, and Billy hollers, "Dude, what are you doing?"

"Food fight!" someone yells.

Jax stomps toward Billy's table and gets in his face. Next thing I know, they're wrestling on the floor. Some kids cheer them on while others scream. I bury my head in my arms. If I don't protect my ears, I'll get swept up in all the noise and carried off to someplace I don't want to be.

A high-pitched whistle cuts through the racket. Principal Wolf plants herself in the middle of the cafeteria, blowing hard into the whistle hanging from her neck. Her black bowl cut sways around her puffed out cheeks. I press my fingers deeper into my ears.

The room grows silent. No one messes with Principal Wolf. She's gigantic. I heard a rumor that she wrestled on a German team before she became a principal.

"Enough! Both of you to the office." Her meaty hands grab Billy and Jax by their collars, and she escorts them out.

Kids whip and whirl around in their seats toward me.

Tick. Tick. Tick.

The second-minute hand on the wall clock taunts me, spinning my head until I feel dizzy. Then, the entire cafeteria erupts into laughter, pointing, whispering—at me. My breath fights fast and shallow. I scramble to pack up the rest of my lunch when I notice Jax's backpack.

I should leave it. I've got enough problems without helping a kid who touches other people's food. Besides, I don't want to miss the after-lunch music class. It's only for fifth-grade girls, and my best chance to meet a friend without boys around. But, halfway to the door, worry sets in. What if someone steals his stuff?

I dart back. The heaviness of his bag presses the strap into my shoulder on the way to the principal's office.

The receptionist peeks over her glasses at me. Her eyes are thin slits cut in half by the top of her tortoise-shell frames. She looks like a lizard. "Can I help you?"

"Ummm, yeah. I have this kid's backpack."

"What's his last name?"

How should I know Jax's last name? "He's got black, curly hair, and acorn—Um, I mean brown eyes?"

She slides the glasses up the bridge of her nose. Her attention returns to the monitor. "Care to be more specific?" *Click-clack* on the keyboard.

I could be a lot more specific. He smells regular. Like a boy. Not a Fancy. And he asks for people's food. Oh, and he wears a big face watch and those basketball shoes, the kind with black rubber soles that leave scuff marks.

"Uhhh, he's kinda tall?" I say, which is true in comparison to me. I'm only four-foot-seven.

Without looking up from her screen, the receptionist flicks her pointer finger at the principal's office. "He'll be in there for a while. Leave it with me."

I peer through Principal Wolf's office door window to see her lecturing Jax and Billy. My arms hug his backpack. Jax whirls around in his chair and looks right at me like he knew I was staring at the back of his head.

He winks.

Did he just—? My legs wobble, and I stumble backward, set to bolt from the room.

"The backpack?" Mrs. Lizard-Face has all eyes on me. She reaches out with her dry, scaly arm.

"Here." I dump his pack on her desk and race away.

"No running in the halls!" Lizard yells after me.

With twenty seconds to spare before the tardy bell rings, I fly through the music class door. My sneakers stick to the floor, and I tumble over my shoes and crash into a music stand, knocking it over. I grab for a desk to stop myself from falling but fall smack on my stomach. A loud fart escapes.

One snicker after another rises in chorus. Alexa stands over me, waving her hand in front of her nose, laughing loudest of all.

Poof. Floss appears in a cloud of powdered sugar, scurrying near Alexa's feet, ready to scrabble up her leg.

"Go away!" I yell and chuck a broken pencil from the floor at her ankle, trying to scare him off.

Jaws drop, and the girls clamber to the other side of the room, far away from me.

The teacher walks in with music books in hand. "What's going on in here?"

My neck flops, and my forehead knocks the tile. Any chance of fifth-grade ordinary sprints out the door.

3

SPITBALLS AND PICKLES

The final bell rings.

I sling my backpack over my shoulder and rush toward the exit, ducking past throngs of kids cluttering the hall, hoping to leave this nightmare of a day behind. But the chaos continues outside. A group of girls stops right in my path, forcing me to swerve onto the grass. When I finally make it to the parking lot, Billy is standing smack in the middle of the walkway. I sidestep and hide behind the crossing sign.

A deep voice yells, "Billy Simpson!"

I peek around the pole.

Billy's dad rushes up the sidewalk and looms over him, shouting and waving his arms. His dad's face puffs out like a Mylar balloon, all crinkled and shiny. The more his dad screams, the more his balloon face shrinks into itself. Then he takes a breath, and his cheeks blow back up for another round.

Billy stares at the sidewalk.

"Boy, I don't have time to come down here to bail your butt

out of trouble," Mr. Proper Simpson says.

"Proper" is not his real name, but it's what Grams calls him. He wears a black suit, like always. He's a lawyer, I think, or something important like that. Mr. Simpson's freckles are the same penny-copper color as Billy's, except they're sort of faded and clumped together.

Will Billy's clump when he gets old?

In kindergarten, Billy had fifty-three freckles, not including the round mole on his chin. I know because we counted them, back when we were friends.

"I lost half a day's work! That's coming out of your allowance."

"But some kid hit me with—"

Mr. Simpson grabs Billy by the collar and drags him toward a white sports car parked diagonally across two spaces. His growl lowers, but I can still hear him. "I don't care what he did. You keep this up, and I'm sending you to live with your grandmother."

For a minute, I feel bad for Billy. He's not nice to me most of the—well, all of the time, but it's no fun being yelled at. My worry for Billy stops when he notices me watching from behind the pole and raises his lip to snarl. I'm sure he'd throw spitballs at me right now if he could get away with it.

The car door slams shut, and Billy keeps throwing eye daggers at me through the window until his dad speeds away. He'd better be careful, or his face might get stuck like that.

I check my watch, a boring digital one, not a cool one with both an hour hand and minute hand like Jax's. *Shoot!* I have less than a minute before the bus leaves without me. I sprint along the line of buses, checking each one for the number. By the time I find bus seventeen, my face is flushed and sweaty.

"Hop on," Mr. Jennings calls out, waving his hand for me to board.

I climb the four steps. There's one seat left. Right beside Jax! *Holy monkeys!* I can't sit by him again. What if he asks for food?

Jax nods to the spot next to him.

This is awkward. Clutching my backpack tight to my chest, I slide down on the bench and sit close to the edge.

He shifts closer and nudges me. "How you doing?"

My shoulders shrug like they're on their own.

"You gonna talk to me?"

I open my mouth, but my throat closes up. I can't speak.

One corner of his mouth slyly tilts up. "Don't worry, everyone farts."

Are you kidding?!? My heart skips, and my face burns hot. I jerk my head around to check if anyone heard. Alexa looks me in the eye and pinches her nose at me. She *told* him! Even after I tried to be helpful and shoo Floss away from her.

"Th-That's rude. You shouldn't talk about fa—" I cover my face with my hands and duck low in the seat, squeezing my head tight to distract me. The trick doesn't work.

"No big deal," Jax says. "Better out then in, my mom says. Gas could blow up your stomach. Make it puff out like a balloon."

"What? Is that true?" I pat circles around my stomach. It feels flat and hungry, not puffy. "You're lying. Leave me alone." I hug my arms tight.

"But—"

"I mean it!" Squeezing my eyes shut, I hum. All I wanted was one friend, but no. Floss and Alexa ruined everything, and now no one will ever help me save Mr. Dally.

"Whatever." Jax scoots toward the window and slumps down, pulling his hoodie over his eyes. The other kids yell over each other and interrupt my humming, making the ride noisy and bumpy all the way home.

At my stop, I hop off the bus. The sun is bright, and all

around me, pollen floats like chinchilla puffs and sticks to lawns and parked cars. "Pickles!" *Ah-choo.* I don't have allergies. My parents even had me tested. Dr. Richter says I have photic sneezing. It runs in families, and Mom swears it comes from Dad's side. But Dr. Richter taught me a trick, to not stare directly into light. If that doesn't work, he told me to say "pickles" to distract me from a sneeze.

Eyes forward, I keep my attention off the sun. I wave to the little girl hopscotching at the corner house where Grams lived before moving in with us. My family has lived here in Michiana, Indiana, for a long time. Dad's flower shop is a few blocks east.

Waiting to cross the street, I hear someone shuffling behind me. I cross and pick up speed; the shuffle quickens. I know how this goes. Bullies always come from behind. My feet pound the pavement faster and faster until I break into a run.

"Hey, Meredith. Slow down!" Jax's long legs matched my pace.

I keep running, gulping in the thick air. "What do you want?"

"I'm just talking to you. What's the big deal?" he says, and not even out of breath.

"I don't want to talk." I stop and gasp for fresh air. "You're rude." My lungs inhale deeper. "And you threw my apple. Now everyone hates me, and now my new name's going to be Mashed-Potato-Hair. You should have stayed out of it."

"Oh. My bad." He studies my hair. "Besides, that's dumb. Your hair doesn't look like mashed potatoes. It's kinda glowy."

Finger combing through my hair, my hand gets caught on a tangle. I slide my hand away from my head and make a quick hop over a crack.

"Still don't like cracks, huh?" Jax laughs and jumps one, too.

"Do I know you?" Only my family and Floss know about me hating cracks. He's probably mistaking me for someone else.

Jax leans down to tie his Converse High Tops. "You don't remember me?"

"We've never met."

"Come on. Seriously?" Jax stands up and narrows his eyes on me. "When we were kids? Before my da—." His face pales. "You know what? Never mind."

"Uh, huh. Well, I better go." I stretch my leg out for a giant step in the other direction. Floss must be behind all this, and no way I'm trusting that lousy beetle. One time he even tricked a boy into sending me a candygram.

"Hold on." Jax catches up to me a few houses down. "I changed my mind. Let's hang out."

I keep walking because I'm not hanging out with him. I've had enough today. I didn't even make a single friend. *Unless I did?* Nope. Jax can't be my new friend. She's supposed to be a girl. Says so on the list. I speed up.

"Come on!" He runs backward to face me. "It'll be fun."

"What would be fun?" I slow a little.

"I'm not sure yet. But if I'm right, *everything*." His face lights up, all mischievous. "How about we go to the park?"

Not happening. I speed back up—the park's where Isabel and Alexa go after school.

"Or the rec center?" He flips around and runs forward to keep up with me. "Some kids are shooting hoops there."

I shake my head. "Don't know how."

"You're kidding?" He stops.

"No." I kick at a dirt clump on the sidewalk and miss.

Jax stares at me and throws up his hands. "Do you even want to be friends?"

My body freezes. I try to remember if I actually did write down that my friend had to be a girl. I chew a fingernail. No. I didn't. Did the plan work? I bite off the fingernail, and I'm still deciding. I guess there's only one way to be sure. "Can we do something I want?"

"Sure. We'll do what you want first."

"Fine, I'll go. But wait here a sec. I need to tell my grandma." Dad says that you should *never* tell strangers where you live.

"Okay." Jax glances at his oversized watch. "Hurry."

My red sneakers hit the sidewalk, and I take off running. To be safe, I check to make sure Jax doesn't see me turn at the corner.

Out of breath, I poke my head in the front door. "Grams, school's done. I'm gonna hang out with some kids." I drop my backpack on the landing.

"Where at?" Grams hollers from upstairs. Jingles, her dog, joins in, barking.

"Around the neighborhood!"

"Okay. Be home before dinner."

I cut through the grass to get back to where I left Jax. Once my feet hit the sidewalk, I leap over cracks. My heart skips along with me. Good thing Grams was home because Mom would have given me the third degree. Maybe my luck's changing.

Now, I need to make sure none of my Fancies scare Jax off, and maybe he'll help me unjinx Mr. Dally.

4

Not Me

Quick as I can, I hurry back to the spot where I left Jax. I'm starting to worry if him asking me to hang out was a tease. What if once I get there, he and his real friends are gone? My arms pump faster, hoping to catch up with him.

Jax is still right where I left him, sitting on the curb, waiting for *me*. It wasn't all a big tease.

"You came back!" He jumps to his feet and punches the air.

My chest warms like my heart's glowing. "But I need to be home before dinner."

"We will. Where do you want to go?"

"Follow me."

"Okay." Jax's brows waggle. "But stay on the lookout. If we see anybody, get super-still. Pretend you're a tree." He stops and holds his arms out like they're branches. "Like this."

Uh-oh. My glow fades and chills to ice. "Like we're real trees?"

"What? No, we pretend. Use our imaginations."

"How about we hide?" I shift one foot to the other. "They'll still see us."

"C'mon, what's wrong with using your imagination?" He keeps his arms out and wiggles his fingers.

But using my imagination is too risky. Fancies might pop out and try to play with us. My memory skims through my "Make a Friend" list to come up with something safer. No luck. The only idea I can think of is, *Do something your new friend wants to do.* So, I "gopher" it and stretch out my arms.

"Yeah, like that." He drops his arms and shakes out his hands.

I drop mine and check around. Nothing's changed. *Whew.*

He taps his watch. "Let's go."

We jump cracks and curbs and dodge between sidewalk trees. Jax keeps swiveling his head, investigating, searching for something. I'm not sure what. He doesn't even stop pretending when cars go by. We freeze with our arms in branch configurations, and the drivers give us strange looks.

We creep from street to street. I finally ask, "What happens if we see other kids?"

Jax stops. "What do you mean?"

"I mean, if anyone from school sees us being trees, they'll think we're weird."

"So. Who cares?" Jax's face scrunches. "We ignore them."

Easy for him to say.

"Misty!" A high-pitched trill comes from the funny cat-neighbor, Ms. Bittle. She scans the street, standing outside her house wearing a pink robe. "Misty! Where are you?"

An orange and black tabby sits on the sidewalk, licking its

paw and completely ignoring Ms. Bittle. The cat stops and gives us a death stare—*bad kitty*. I should know. One time, Misty threw up a foam wad containing a grasshopper all over my lap. Ms. Bittle said that if a cat throws up on you, it's a sign of good luck. It didn't feel lucky.

"Meredith, is that you?" Ms. Bittle turns toward us and shades her eyes.

I freeze.

Jax jumps in front of me and poses with his arms spread out wide.

"Meredith? Is Misty over there?"

Jax slowly unfreezes and moves into another weird tree angle. No way Ms. Bittle's going to mistake him for a moving tree. Coughing, Jax calls out in a garbled, deep voice. "No! No Meredith here. No Misty either!"

Should I pose? I extend my arms and stand on my tiptoes to make myself taller. My toes cramp. Just when I don't think I can stay on my toes much longer, Jax whispers, "Go!"

We race to the street corner and burst out laughing. Jax's laugh makes me laugh harder, not because it's a funny laugh, or a snort, or anything like that—but because we are both laughing. Then, I feel bad. "We should have got Misty home."

"That cat doesn't need any help."

"How do you know?"

"Because Misty's there for Ms. Bittle, not the other way around."

For some reason, I get what he's saying. Jingles helps Grams too.

We return to playing trees. I'm not sure how long we

jump cracks and dodge cars when we cross the busy street in front of McNally's market. The farther we venture from my neighborhood, the more the houses look familiar. I've been here before. It's not my block, but I speed past Jax and go left. Six houses down, I make another left.

Jax catches up. "Do you know where you're going?"

"Yes." But I don't know why I came this way. The Dally's house is on the other block.

I stop in front of a red and white brick house the size of a small hotel with four big garage doors attached to the side. I kneel and touch the freshly mowed grass; the soft green blades tempt me to roll around the same way Jingles does on lawns and carpets. This house is enormous, beautiful enough to cover the front of Grams' garden magazines—except for the rose bushes lining the patio. Every one of them is nothing more than a clump of dried-up stems and thorns.

I stand and turn to Jax. "Follow me."

We creep up along the side of the lawn to the patio and crouch behind the dismal bushes. I'm pretty sure they're not hiding us at all. The shutters are wide open, so I peer over the brittle branches into the windows. Inside, Billy sits alone on a white couch facing a gigantic TV screen.

I've sat on that couch before, more than once. Back when the patio roses bloomed with beautiful, lush petals. Billy's mom and mine were friends, making us "sort-of friends." That was until second grade when he announced to the whole class I played with pretend friends. He couldn't see the Fancies.

My arms shiver with goosebumps. "This is Billy Simpson's house. I used to come here."

"Because you're friends?" Jax's voice quickens.

"Not anymore."

He wrings his hands. "But you could be, right?"

"No." I shoot him a sharp look. "Why?"

"Because we need to be friends with Billy."

"No."

"Come on, Dandy—"

"Stop calling me Dandy!" I stand up and stomp my foot in the dirt. "My name's Meredith. And I don't have to be friends with anyone. You don't know Billy. He'd probably want us to jinx Ms. Bittle's house and ruin her life, too." I storm off, not caring who sees me.

Jax cuts in front of me to walk backward. "Why would we jinx anyone?"

"You don't get it. Billy's mean."

"Right. But who believes in jinxes anyway?"

"I do!" I cross my arms. Clouds block the sun, and my teeth chatter. This plan isn't turning out so good. Jax can't be my friend if he doesn't believe me. I spin around and trek back toward McNally's.

"Wait. Don't go. I didn't mean anything," Jax says. "I'm just saying—oh, never mind." He pulls off his black hoodie. "Here, take this."

"No."

"You're cold. Don't be stubborn."

"I'm not stubborn."

"Okay. Fine. Tell me about this jinx thing."

"You sure?"

He holds out his jacket. "Yep. I want to know."

Mashed potato splatter crusts the hoodie. My shivers prod me to take it anyway. Hesitantly, I slip my arms into the sleeves and tuck my hands into the fleece-lined pockets. I stick my nose into the jacket collar and sniff. It smells like Jax—sandalwood deodorant and sweat. The goosebumps retreat.

My lips smile without me even trying. "Okay. But first, you need to see *the situation.*"

We take off to the next block. Another street down, we cross at the corner. Next thing I know, we're almost directly in front of the Dally's. I dig in my heels on the sidewalk before I cross over the boundary of the ghostly grey house. Dust pollution swarms around the Dally's porch and chokes out the flowers. They're dead. I mean *dead, dead.* Skeleton vines cling to the wall; the leafless claws barely hold where they creep up the bricks.

I shield my eyes, then slowly spread my fingers. The sun peeks through the cracks. "Pickles!"

Jax takes a step to pass me on the sidewalk.

"Wait! What are you doing?" I scramble my arms forward and grab hold of his sleeve before he crosses over to the next section of sidewalk.

He tugs his arm from my grip. "What are you doing?"

"Saving your life." With one hand, I point at the house while the other grasps his elbow. "Why do you think it's called 'Dead Man's Castle?'"

Jax rolls his eyes. "It's just a house."

My jaw drops. "Not true. I mean, it's not technically a castle, but it is jinxed. And probably haunted."

He frowns. "So, what, we can't go on the sidewalk in front of it?"

Usually, I would cross the street and stay on the other side, but I remember my checklist. *Teach a friend something new.* Dr. Richter says it's not helpful to tell someone how to do something. Show them. Since Jax doesn't know how to use the jinx-blocker for protection, he might get mixed up in something terrible. Who knows what. If it's the same thing as Mr. Dally, Jax may never leave his house again.

"Okay, Jax. Watch me and do what I do. Don't change a single thing." I cover my left eye and speedwalk past the house repeating, "Not me, not me, not me."

The blocker works. Jax is right behind me when we hit the other side.

"Cool. Did you make that up?" he asks.

"No. Why would I make up something so horrible?" I drop to the curb to stop shaking. "This isn't right. Mr. Dally doesn't deserve to be jinxed. He's the nicest man ever."

Jax glimpses back at the house. "This is the Dally's home?"

"Of course, it is!" But I can't blame him for not knowing. He's the new kid. "Mr. and Mrs. Dally were a nice older couple who used to grow vegetables for everyone in town. They even competed in the Indiana Harvest Festival for the biggest squash competition, and they won three years in a row," I say, so proud of them.

"What happened?"

"Everything." My voice reduces to a whisper. "This summer, I was on my way over to help them make an apple cake. There were fire trucks and an ambulance outside. The neighbor said Mrs. Dally died."

His face slacks. "That's bad."

"The worst." My eyes sting with tears. "They were my friends. I used to help in their garden, and they gave me fresh zucchini to take home to my dad." I point toward a fenced-off patch of dirt under their oak tree. "Over there used to be a front yard garden. Now, he doesn't even water it."

Jax squints at the dirt. "Why?"

"I don't know. No one's seen Mr. Dally since his wife died." My arms shiver, and I hug myself tight. "But I saw him in the upstairs window. His face is grey and droopy." I fumble for the right words. "He might be the living dead, a zombie."

"A zombie?"

"I've tried, you know, to break the jinx. N-nothing's worked."

Jax chews off a cuticle.

"It's all Billy's fault!"

"The jinx? Aw, get off it. How could Billy be involved?"

"Because he ruins everything. Now, Billy's jinx can't be broken, and Mr. Dally's stuck inside his house all alone. He doesn't have anyone anymore. It's not fair."

"And you're sure Billy did all this?" Jax swirled his hand around to indicate the Dally's house and garden, then back to me.

"Yes. He even told everyone he did it. And why are you sticking up for him anyway? You two got into a fight."

"We didn't get into a fight. I mean, not a real fight."

"Tell Principal Wolf." I huff.

"She sure has a good grip." Jax grabs the scruff of his shirt collar and spins around in a circle, pretending he's chained to a leash. He stops and collapses on the sidewalk, then glances up at me. "I didn't mean to get in trouble. I was trying to figure out if Billy remembers he's one of us."

"We're not an *us* to be one of. He's a bully. Billy's not one of anybody. You must be confused."

"I'm not confused. You are. *I* still remember who I am." Jax stands, grumpy, and brushes the dust off his jeans.

"You're not making sense." I'm not sure why he's angry, but it makes me mad. "I know who I am!" I pull off his hoodie and hurl it at him. "I don't need your help anyway. I'm going home."

He catches the jacket midair. "Fine."

"And don't follow me." I take off and don't stop running until I get to the corner of my street. The whole time, my feet pound the cement, like two hollow stumps clomping down a sleepy street.

Shivering, I walk to my driveway. For a quick moment, I wish I didn't give Jax back his jacket. But I had to. It's not mine, and keeping something would be stealing, which would make me a bad friend.

My head drops. Mrs. Dally would be so disappointed in me, and not just because of Jax. I haven't been a good friend to Mr. Dally. He would never be afraid to visit someone. Even when I had the flu, Dad told them I was contagious, but Mr. Dally didn't care. He and Mrs. Dally brought over green apples and told me to eat one a day to keep the doctor away, and it did.

I'm a bad friend. *No.* A terrible friend.

5

GUMMI BEARS

Jingles is there to meet me when I walk through the door. Wagging his bushy dog tail, he jumps on me, almost knocking me over, and flashes his toothy smile.

"Down, boy," I tell him, but he hardly listens to Dad or me. Only Grams and Mom. Mainly because he's stubborn and his hearing's wonky. I suggested hearing aids. Dad says Jingles doesn't need them; he hears the word "treat" just fine. He's a rescue Grams adopted the year I was born. Put in dog jail, "falsely accused of ripping up shoes."

I try again. "Down!"

His long, pink tongue slobbers my face.

I give in, sprawling on the floor to scratch behind his floppy ears. Jingles sniffs my jean pockets, then races to the base of the stairs and sniffs my backpack, looking for Floss. They have a love/chase relationship.

"Floss better not be in there, after what he pulled today," I say and get up from the floor.

Jingles tilts his head at me and paws my pack.

"You're back early," Grams calls from the kitchen. "How was your day?"

"Perfect." Our code word for *totally sucked*.

Bored with the backpack, Jingles follows right on my heels into the kitchen.

"Bad, huh? Sounds like a milkshake kind of day." Grams pulls ice cream from the freezer and drags her step stool to the counter. She uses the stool for everything. Dad teases that she's as short as she is feisty. With her extra height, she towers over the blender and scoops creamy white blobs into it. Then she adds a splash of milk.

Once the motor stops, she offers me the milkshake. Vanilla. My favorite. I take a large swallow. My brain freezes, and my hand flies to my forehead.

She gives me those kind Grams eyes and drops a handful of Gummi Bears in the blender before hitting the button. "Any nice kids?" she hollers over the loud motor.

I stick my tongue to the roof of my mouth to unfreeze it before answering, "Maybe."

Grams shuts off the blender and scoops the remaining shake into her cup. A rainbow of colorful bears chopped to bits swims in the ice cream. Bear-globs climb up her clear straw, and she chews them to pieces before swallowing. "We should start planning your birthday party."

"Not having one."

"Sure, you are." She climbs off the stool. "Or would you prefer a surprise party? I could invite your friends."

The surprise would be on Grams. The only people who'd show up would be her, my parents, and Jingles. I'd be surrounded by my family, wearing some colorful birthday hat, holding a balloon, and blowing out eleven candles. Floss might crash the party for cake. *Would Jax come?*

I take another sip of my shake. No. I'm not having a party. I can't take another year of my parents pretending they're not disappointed when no one shows up. Besides, I need to concentrate on Mr. Dally.

"I'm going to my room," I tell Grams and head upstairs.

I grab my backpack on the way up and slide the journal out once I shut my bedroom door. I count the ideas I'd wasted trying to make a friend. Three because of Floss. Four spent on Jax, who probably hates me now. Nineteen left—an odd number. My stomach lurches. I rustle inside the pack, scavenging for a pen to add an idea to the list, so it'll be even, but I stop. Adding anything new would be cheating. But would it, really?

No. It would.

I toss the backpack on the dresser and open to the *"Make a Friend"* page, reciting the first idea not yet checked off on the list. *"Introduce yourself and compliment the new people you meet."*

I thrust my hand at the mirror. "Hi. I'm Meredith Smart. I like your hair." Well, that's a lie. All I see is myself with broken strands of cotton hair trying to shake hands back. I grab some hair gel and dab the goo on my hands. Working it through the uncooperative strands only makes things a million times worse. Now my hair resembles a scraggly kitten, its fur plastered down from over-licking.

But I try again. "Hey. I'm Mere. What's your name?" I flick my hand through my hair and jut out my hip.

My reflection frowns and sticks out her tongue.

Great. I can't even be friends with myself. *Ugggh!* I stomp to the bathroom.

Floss dancing and jiggling on the sink. He races around the bathroom counter while I lather up my hands to wash off the goop. I'm still mad about him showing up at school, so I ignore him.

Plfffff. He blows raspberries at me.

I rinse my hands and twist off the faucet, reaching for the plastic mouthwash cup, raising it to a hover. "Gotcha!" I slam the cup over Floss and press my ear to the container.

I hear scratching. "I'm not going to hurt you," I tell him.

The scratching stops. But I don't trust Floss. "If you would show yourself to people, this whole mess would be over."

A muffled "I'm dying" cough followed by a gagging noise comes from inside the cup.

"You're fine."

Thump. Something hits against the plastic.

My heart drops.

No. It's a trick.

Just in case, I lift the cup's edge and look for Floss. He's not there. I pick up the container and shake it out—empty. I catch a glimpse of the thieving beetle scurrying across the floor toward my bedroom.

"No, you don't!" I hurl myself through the bathroom door and leap, landing smack on the carpet—Floss snickers and dashes into a wall hole. Jumping to my feet, I slam the cup against the wall. "I know you're real!"

"Meredith?" Mom yells from downstairs. "Are you okay?"

"I'm fine!" I yell back, kicking the bed.

"Owww-oww-owww!" I drop the cup and grab my stubbed toe. "Now look what you did. You no good, sneaky—" I stomp, sending sharp pains up my leg. "Leave me alone, Floss. I mean it."

I whip around and spy the *Summer Girl* magazine tossed open on the nightstand. I snatch it and jump on the bed. My body sinks heavy into the mattress, and I flip through pages for free lipstick and perfume samples. An article with colorful pictures stops me. "Summer Break Ideas." On the page, kids ride bikes, camp at sleepovers, and swim at the beach. They look happy together.

If I could just figure out their secret.

I focus on a picture of girls playing sand volleyball and try to imagine *me* inside the magazine with a best friend on the beach.

Kssch. Kssch. Beetle feet click across the ceiling.

"Stop it," I tell him without looking up, but I know he doesn't care. Floss wants me miserable.

I study the beach picture. There has to be a clue somewhere on the pages, but my lashes start to feel heavy.

Yawning, I hear seagulls squawking overhead. Then, I see her—a girl about my age—wearing a yellow swimsuit. She smiles and waves me over. The sun's warmth further entices me, and the girl and I race to each other across the sand. She's within an arm's reach when a thick mist rolls in and washes out my vision.

"Hold on!" I cry and stretch out my hand. Warm saltwater splashes my cheeks. My chest constricts, and I'm left standing alone, waist-deep in the ocean with waves crashing down all around me, pounding me into the sand. The salty water seeps into my mouth—choking me. I want to open my eyes and escape, but then I'll never find my new friend again.

My lids twitch, but I fight to keep them closed, squeezing them tight. My lashes flutter and the dam holding back my tears bursts. The yellow bathing suit girl dissipates like raindrops washed her into the colorful magazine pages.

No one's ever going to be my friend.

Cheek pressing against the tear-stained page, I sob, wishing my heart would burst into a million grains of sand.

Because then, I wouldn't care anymore.

6

WHITE MOTH

Dad strolls through the door at six o'clock. Tonight, he's carrying a single purple rose.

"Hey, kiddo," he says and pecks me on the cheek before announcing, "I'm home!" for everyone else to hear. He replaces the yellow rose in the bud vase on the table in the foyer. Dad brings a rose to Mom every night. Being a flower nursery owner has perks.

Grams bustles in from the kitchen and leans in behind him to inspect the flower. She knows flowers. That's how she made a living, selling plants from her backyard greenhouse. Dad got his horticulture passion from her. Grams still jokes that he sold his first petunia from his crib.

"Do you think she'll like it?" Dad plucks a single, less-than-perfect petal before stepping away from the table.

Before Grams can answer, Mom swoops in from the kitchen, her baby-blue maxi dress swaying behind her. "It's beautiful." Mom could be a model, which she would love. Clothes are her thing. She looks nothing like me. A perfect rose, Dad calls her. Or he used to before they started worrying about me. Recently, she took a job at Val's, the neighborhood clothing store, and gets the best discounts.

Mom sniffs the flower and raises her brow. "This one smells stronger."

"Good." He clears his throat, and Grams pats his shoulder. Usually, he'd close in on Mom with a hug and kiss her cheek. Tonight, he doesn't. Their fighting has been getting worse. No chance I'm asking for any additional ketchup packets tomorrow.

Grams looks back and forth between my parents. "Supper's almost ready." As she leads us into the kitchen, she says to Mom, "Isn't it interesting how scents hold our memories? One sniff is all it takes to remember a special person or time." Grams loves scents. She says smells that trigger memories are more potent than sight or sound—and that's why she doesn't own a camera.

I believe her. Whenever I get a whiff of pine, it reminds me of Christmas way more than any of Mom's holiday photo albums.

Mom opens the silverware drawer and pulls out four forks and four butter knives. "Did you meet any new friends in school?"

"Not really," I mumble, and Grams glances at me sideways.

Dad grits his teeth. "Cassandra, we agreed to let it go."

She bumps the drawer closed with her hip and stiffly sets the table. "No. *You* agreed."

My heart thumps, heavy and hollow. I want to tell her about Jax to stop the inevitable fight in its track. But he's no longer my friend.

Dad grabs a potholder and yanks the oven door open. "For one day, can we stick to the plan?" Standing in front of the hot oven, he sways slightly, willowy—I look like him more than Mom. He pulls out the casserole and sets it on Grams' tulip-shaped trivet next to the stovetop.

Ring. Ring.

We all stop and stare at the home phone attached to the wall. I don't even know why we have a landline. The only calls we ever get on that number are from telephone solicitors.

Dad tugs off the oven mitt and answers using his singsong voice. "Hello."

Mom rolls her eyes. For some reason, he'll talk to salespeople like he's their best friend. Drives her bonkers.

"Who is this?" Dad's voice deepens. He covers the receiver. "Hey, kiddo, it's for you." He holds the phone out to me.

"Who is it?" I whisper.

He rubs his chin. "Jax?"

Oh, holy monkeys! I want to take the phone, but I can barely breathe. Shaking my head and backing away, I bump into the kitchen table. A glass tips over and splashes milk all over the tile floor. Jingles rushes over to lap up the spill.

"No, Jingles!" Mom squeals in her flurry for a towel.

Dad puts the phone back up to his ear. "Jax, she can't come to the phone right now. She's too busy tearing up the kitchen."

I flail my arms and signal him to stop talking.

He grins. "Now, she's landing a plane."

I cross my arms and glare at him.

"Sure, I'll tell her. Goodbye."

Soon as he hangs up, I yell, "I can't believe you said that!"

"Why? I should say even more to any boy calling my ten-year-old daughter."

"I'm almost eleven."

"Phillip, really!" Mom finishes wiping up the milk. "Why would you tease her and make her even more nervous?"

Dad ignores her. "How do you know him? School?"

"No," I say. "From the zoo." Grams refers to the school as "the zoo."

Mom squeezes out the rag over the sink. "See, Phillip? She knows him from school. I'm sure they're just friends. Right, Mere?"

"I—" My chest tightens. Jumbled words stick in my throat, suffocating me. My anger makes it near impossible to breathe. Jax didn't believe me about Billy or the jinx. What gives him the right to go and make my parents argue worse?

I throw up my arms and storm out of the kitchen. "I'm going to bed."

Dad hollers, "But it's only seven o'clock."

In a hushed tone, Grams says, "Let her go, Phillip. She's had an exhausting day. I can bring her food upstairs later."

As I head to the stairs, the foundation of the house shakes like an earthquake hit. But as soon as I hit the landing, I realize I'm the one trembling. How dare Jax call me? And where did he get my number?

I fly up the floral runner centered on the staircase, taking two steps at a time. Then, I race to the room, slamming the door shut behind me. I pounce on my bed and roll up in my comforter like a pig in a blanket. After a moment, I feel myself calming down. Cocooned inside my floral comforter with flowers so big I'm microscopic—a white moth buried within a valley of lilies. My breathing evens out, and I focus on my lavender walls, lavender sheets, and lavender pillowcase—everything in here is lavender. I scowl. I've told Mom over and over that I want posters for my walls. I'm old enough. But the answer is always "no." She insists we keep the walls bare to look fresh and clean.

Throwing off the comforter, I shuffle through a drawer and find an old magazine. I rip off the cover with a random girl on it and thumbtack her to the wall. There! She's my new friend.

Then, I grab my journal and shred my checklist into pieces.

7

FIREFLIES

Tink . . .

Tink . . .

Tink . . .

My eyes fly open. Must've fallen asleep—the bedroom's dark, except for the streetlamp shining through the curtain crack. On my bedside table sits a meager peanut butter sandwich with no crusts and some chips. When I sit up and wipe drool off my face, I spot the mangled journal in the trashcan beside the table.

An ache sinks deep into my bones. All I can think about is poor Mr. Dally. He had the bad luck to get stuck knowing me.

I snatch my pillow and press it against my face.

My cheeks flush hot like the day I met the Dallys, the day from the popsicle stick photo. I remember every detail, my family loading plants into the van that morning, preparing to leave for Indiana's Summer Harvest Fest.

I was upstairs, brushing my hair in the bedroom mirror. Floss nudged hairclips across the top of the dresser. It was annoying, but at least he was behaving. The next thing I knew, that thieving beetle scuttled off with my favorite yellow barrette. I chased him out of the house, past the van out front, then down our block to the Dallys. Floss tried to hide by scurrying up a tree in the Dally's front yard.

I stressed on their sidewalk. I'd been there before with my dad, delivering flowers, but I knew better than to trudge into someone's yard without permission.

Mr. and Mrs. Dally were drinking ice tea and tending to their front garden. Mrs. Dally spotted me and rushed over. She knelt and placed a soft hand on my shoulder. Mr. Dally peered down on me with kind eyes. I told them all about Floss stealing my barrette.

Mr. Dally nodded, not even acting like there was anything odd about chasing a beetle. He helped me search until we found the barrette in the dirt beneath their oak tree.

After that day, my parents let me help in the Dally's garden— twice a week, for two hours at a time. Mrs. Dally paid me in zucchini, and my dad would make me his famous zucchini bread— with chocolate chips, but no nuts, special for me.

As for my mom, Dad would make her a special loaf, one with toasted walnuts. He wrapped the bread in aluminum foil and tied the package with a red ribbon.

I miss the happy-not-fighting, zucchini-bread version of Mom and Dad.

Now, it's been two months since Mrs. Dally died, and everything has changed.

Massaging between my brows to clear my stuffy head, I stumble from bed and fish the ripped journal pages from the trash can. I put the bits of paper in my desk drawer. I'll deal with them later. My stomach growls, and I take a corner bite of my sandwich.

My shoulders slump at the memory of that day with the Dallys. I don't even deserve stale peanut butter. I dump the sandwich in the trash and crawl back in bed, seeking comfort under the warm sheets.

Tink . . . Tink.

I peer up. Sometimes, the metal pulley-thing gets wrapped in the ceiling fan and makes an annoying sound, but the fan is off.

TINK!

There! Something bounces off the window.

I push away the blankets and topple to the floor, creeping over on hands and knees. Pulling myself up at the windowsill, I conceal myself with the curtain panel and peer down at our front yard. I groan. Jax waves up at me from under our old willow tree with a goofy expression on his face. I should ignore him. It's late.

Tink! Tink!

Ugh, but he's not going away.

I throw the curtain aside, revealing myself, and open the window. "What do you want?"

"Come down." Jax disappears behind the tree trunk.

"No, I'm not coming down. What are you doing here?"

He pops his head out, so all I see is his mop of black hair. "What was I supposed to do? You wouldn't take my call."

I close the window halfway when Jax yells, "We need to talk."

"No, we don't!" I scan the room for something to throw at him. This whole miserable day is crashing down on me, and I fall to the floor.

"Mere?" Jax's voice floats through the window.

"Go away," I whisper and curl up in a ball. The pity in Jax's voice smothers me in a blanket of reminders—I'm a failure. A big zero. All I needed to do was make one friend to help me with Mr. Dally and for my parents to be okay. I feel sorry for whichever parent gets stuck with me in the divorce.

I don't want a friend anymore. I'll mess that up, too.

"Come down, Mere! I'll wait right here." Jax goes quiet.

I pick at my fingernail, remembering the fun we had today. Well, before Billy messed everything up. Now, I'm worried. What if Jax is my last shot for help? Pressing my palms to the floor, I push up to my knees and peek out the window. "Okay. I'll come down. Wait right there."

Hope flashes within, and I pause to check myself in the dresser mirror. My ratty hair sticks up like a cotton swab that Jingles chewed up and left on the floor. Jax was wrong. Nothing about my hair is "glowy."

Finger combing flyaway strands down, I smear on some lip balm Grams gave me—the one that smells like peaches—

and sneak down the stairs. The house is silent except for the grandfather clock ticking in the living room. Jingles isn't on his dog bed, which is good because he would bark.

I ease open the front door and tiptoe outside. I can't see Jax.

"Where are you?" I whisper, padding over the wet grass.

My shoulders sag. Here I am, sneaking out, and Jax won't even answer. Just as I'm about to head back inside, I hear a low growl that ends with a hiss. Spinning around, I come face-to-face with Jax hanging upside down from our tree's sturdiest branch, his black curls looser but not standing on end.

I tilt my head to get a better look at him. "What are you doing?"

"I'm an opossum."

"What?" My vision darts around the yard for something to use for protection. A girl can never be too careful. There's a garden hose wrapped up, and I inch toward it, unsure what to do when I get my hands on it. *Could I tie him to the tree?* If I were a cowgirl, it would be my lasso.

I grab the hose and point the nozzle at Jax. "Stay right there!"

"Or what? You gonna spray me?" He drops from the tree and rolls onto his feet. A sly smirk expands across his face.

"I might." I glance back at the spigot, too far away to turn on.

He lifts his hands in the air. "Okay. I give up."

"Good." I drop the hose and square off my shoulders. "How do you know where I live?"

Jax puts his hands in his pockets and looks down. Even under the dim glow from the streetlights, I detect a flush creeping up his face. "If I told you, would you believe me?" he says.

My body tenses. "Did you follow me?"

"No."

"Why should I trust you?"

"I uhhh . . ."

"Forget it." I whirl around and stomp toward the house.

"Because I'm going to help you," Jax says.

I stop in my tracks. "You are?"

"Yep."

I turn around and put my hands on my hips. "I told you, I'm not being friends with Billy."

Jax bends over and picks a blade of grass. "This isn't about him. I mean, not really. The plan is bigger." He sticks the grass tip in his mouth and waggles his brows. "Much bigger. You want to break the jinx, right?"

My hand presses to my mouth, and I nod.

"We're going to be partners, you and I, and we're going to break the jinx."

"You swear?" I don't want to get too excited, but my heart has other plans and speeds up.

"I swear."

My toes tingle with numbness, forcing me to rock on my heels. Ideas race through my mind. "Do you have a plan? I've tried everything."

"This is the part you won't like. You said Billy created the jinx, right?"

"He did."

"Then we need to make friends with Billy. Since he made the jinx, he might know how to break it."

I wring my hands. "There has to be another way."

"Well, there might be—" Jax presses his lips together and

shakes his head. "No. Forget it. You'll think I'm weird."

"I won't. Tell me."

"You sure?"

"Yes."

He draws in a long breath and nods at the light post in front of our house. It's the one that shines directly into my bedroom window. "Check the light post. Real close. What do you see?"

"A light."

He groans. "Mere, try again. This time use that *special thing* you got."

How does he . . . *Wait.* Is Jax like me? I need to find out, so I blink hard. When I open my eyes, the bulb inside the light post flickers and goes dark. A swarm of fireflies twinkles and illuminates the inside of the lamp, where the light bulb went out. They swirl and dance, and I can't stop staring.

One of the fireflies escapes the lamp post and zooms close enough for me to see her waving. She's so miniature and cute—I can't help but wave back. She giggles and returns to the others, adding to the light source in the glass globe.

Jax claps his hands together in triumph. "I knew it!"

"You can see them?" *Ugggh.* What's wrong with me? Of course, he can't see the fireflies. He's messing with me.

Jax leans against the tree, grinning. "I see the same as you see."

Maybe he is like me?

No, he's not. The last time kids pretended to see Floss, they were lying. I'm not playing this game, not again. I cross my arms. "So, you see a light post."

"No—"

The porch light comes on, and Grams steps out the front door. "Mere? What are you doing outside?" Curlers in her hair, she pulls her robe tighter around her body. Jingles pushes past and sniffs the air right beside her. He barks. "No. Shush!" Grams sternly points her finger at him, and he sits with a growl-mumble.

"I came outside to talk to my—" I can't decide if I should call Jax a friend.

He steps forward and waves at Grams. "Hi. I'm a friend of Dand—Mere's. From school. My name's Jax."

"What are you doing out this late, young man?" Grams eyes him suspiciously.

"I had to run to the store for my mom. I live down the street."

"Who's your mom?" She wraps her robe tighter.

"Dalila. Dalila Cooper."

"Were you the young man who called earlier?"

"Yes, Ma'am."

Grams nods and pats Jingles on the head. "Let's go back in." She says to me, "Wrap it up. Five minutes. Even tulips close up at night." She shuts the door and leaves the porch light on.

"She's nice." Jax turns and sniffs at me. "You smell like peaches."

I rub my lips together and get a whiff of the balm. "Are your parents going to be mad you're out late?"

"Nah. My mom's sleeping."

"What about your dad?"

"I don't talk about him." His jaw clenches, and he covers the face of his watch with his hand.

I get it. Sometimes I don't want to talk about my mom either. "So, how do we break the jinx?"

"Meet me after school tomorrow. I've got an idea."

"Tomorrow? What do I tell my parents?"

The porch lights flicker on and off—Grams's signal that my time is short.

"Tell them we're going to the park after school," Jax says. "That's where we'll start."

I stand there, trying to remember the warning signs for "stranger danger." Is Jax a stranger if Grams knows his name and he goes to my school?

Jax pulls the hood on his black hoodie over his head. "If you're out, fine. Be lame. But if you're in, meet me at our lunch table. Think about it. We could have a cool adventure." He turns on his sneakered heels and heads down the street.

I slip back into the house and turn off the porch lights. The lights inside are off, so I take the darkness as a sign Grams isn't mad. Otherwise, she'd be sitting in her comfy chair, waiting to speak with me. Before closing the front door all the way, I take one more look outside to see Jax waving goodbye from the end of the street. My belly flutters, like blowflies playing tag inside my stomach. I lock the door. I'm so excited, I almost trip going up the stairs. Jax and I are a team. *We're going to help you, Mr. Dally.*

Before climbing back in bed, I open the curtains and stare outside, watching the show of fireflies swirling and dancing from inside the light post on the street. They flit around in a choreographed pattern that I recognize. It's been so long since I've seen them that I almost forgot how beautiful they are.

I start to close the curtains but catch sight of a light sparking away from the fireflies. It flares into a rainbow. Suddenly, an odd hummingbird appears with tiny wings that shimmer in the moonlight. I press my nose to the window. *Is that bird wearing a top hat?* I have an odd sense that somehow the bird is . . . *familiar.*

I lift my hand to wave, but my brain fizzes like a soda can burst open inside my skull. I pull my hand back and pull the curtains together. *No.* I can't do this anymore. The fireflies—they're not real.

My heart disagrees. *Yes, they are.*

8

Bus Seat Jumper

Trash collectors slam our cans against their compacting dumpster and wake me. A yawn snaps my mind to attention.

The fireflies! Untangling my feet from the sheets, I hop out of bed and yank open the curtains. I beat the sun, but the streetlight is dark. No fireflies.

"Please, please, please . . ." I gaze out the window at the now-ordinary lamp post. Maybe if I wish hard enough, I won't see Fancies ever again. I need to do real things with real friends, like break the jinx with Jax.

Pots and pans crash and bang downstairs. I whip through the closet and go through a stack of shirts. Every top has some cuddly animal on the front. I choose one with bunnies and pull on my favorite jeans. Today, they have some give, but it's only day number two. One of Mom's latest house rules: no wearing clothes more than two days in a row. She doesn't like it when my jeans are stretched out. She says they make me look messy, which reminds me to fix my hair. I brush through tangles and add a white hairband.

Holy monkeys! The band disappears into my snowy hair. I toss it and snap on a silver barrette instead.

The scent of warm butter and maple syrup greets me halfway down the stairs. *Yum!* Today's going to be the best day ever. My stomach growls and spurs me into the kitchen where Dad stands at the stove wearing the chef hat I made for his birthday. Grams is next to him, helping make breakfast. Dad's the best chef I know. He comes up with the craziest inventions. My two favorites are his cereal French toast and his peanut butter and bacon waffles. French toast is what's in the pan this morning.

When I was little, Grams told me Dad read everything he could find on Supertasters and slowly introducing textures and flavors. It worked. I eat more things, but Dad's cooking is the only food I trust without Heinz ketchup.

Everyone loves his cooking. Grams also says if he ever quits the flower business, he'd make a perfect television chef. He could call himself "Chef Fill-Up," which she thinks is clever. But Mom says Phillip is such a common name that most people wouldn't get it.

Dad flips a French toast. "Good morning."

"New shirt?" Grams asks. *Did she tell him that Jax came over last night?*

"Where's Mom?" I shift from one foot to the other.

"She had an early morning."

Best. Day. Ever. Dad never asks questions like Mom. I pop a blueberry in my mouth and sit on the barstool across from them. "Can I go to the park after school?"

"What's at the park?" Grams asks.

"Some kids." I act like I don't care.

Dad puts an extra pat of butter in the pan, and it sizzles. "Any kids I know?"

"No. They're from school."

"Will the zoo kid be there?" Dad asks.

"Jax." I roll my eyes. "His name's Jax."

"Jacks?" His mouth quirks. "Like the game with the red ball?"

"No. The cleaner, Ajax, but without the A."

"Okay, then." He chuckles. "So, is the cleaner kid going to the park today, too?"

"He's not a cleaner, Dad!"

"Fine." He turns down the burner. "Will Ajax, without the A, be at the park?"

"I don't know." A knot clumps in my throat, and I scuff the side of the counter with my tennis shoes. I'm not great at lying. "He might be."

Grams cocks her head and raises her orange brows so high they touch her hairline.

"One or two?" Dad asks, holding out a stack of French toast.

"One."

"Two it is." He winks and slides a plate in front of me.

"So, can I go?"

"Don't see why not. Make sure you're home when the streetlights come on."

"Okay." I don't know why Dad thinks it's nighttime by the streetlights. We have clocks. My stomach grumbles, and I dunk my French toast in a separate syrup dish, gobbling down two slices before I have to leave for the bus.

I practically skip to the bus stop. I'm so excited that my toes press down, and my feet hop higher off the ground.

But then . . . *pop-crack-spark.* Plants sprout out from the sidewalk cracks in front of me. They blossom into flowers of all assorted colors. Floral perfume fills the air.

Holy monkeys, not now!

"You're my imagination," I tell them. The rainbow of flowers ignores me and keeps sprouting, forming a colorful line to the bus stop. *Why did Jax have to bring up the fireflies?* Now, it's starting all over again. I jump over the flowers and hum loudly. I know better than to pay any attention to them. They're like Billy—more attention only makes things worse.

The humming finally works. The flowers wither and disappear back into the cracks.

"Poof! Be gone," I say with a giggle. *See,* I can control this.

At the bus stop, crowds of kids are waiting. Now, I have stomach butterflies, and they are in a flurry. Dr. Richter says butterflies represent an emotion. But my butterflies don't feel like an emotion. Mine are probably moths.

Instead of worrying, I count the hours that Jax and I have been friends. Almost a day. How long do we need to be friends before I can ask him to my birthday party? What if he says yes? I could have a party at the new pizza place or the movies. I don't have enough friends for a big party to cost my parents too much. Except, the other kids might want to come because Jax does.

I start counting how many kids are at the stop. I should

know how many potential friends there are here. *Sixteen*. An even number. For my birthday, I could ask for a party instead of gifts.

I had been planning to ask for a phone, but I'm not holding my breath. Mom's argued against that whole idea for years. She says kids get their heads stuck in them. But everyone has them. And if she wants me to have friends, and everyone else's heads are stuck in them, who do I talk to?

Most kids from my school got their phones last year. There was a fire drill at school, and some kids wandered off and didn't go back to their classrooms when it was over. The school panicked and made calls to the parents, which scared them half to death. The next day everyone had a phone—except me—changing school forever with a wave of silence, except for thumbs *tap, tap, tapping* under the desks. No matter how hard I try, I can't ignore the tapping. No one else seems to notice.

The bus pulls up. I fly up the steps and sit in the middle of a bench, saving a seat for Jax.

The next stop is Billy's. He sits two rows in front of me and flicks the kid's ear in front of him without even checking to see if Mr. Jennings is watching. Billy's not afraid of anyone. Jax's plan better be good, something that doesn't involve getting either one of us beaten up by Billy.

At the last stop, Jax hops on. I scoot over and wait for him to sit, but he brushes right past me, his hands jammed in his pockets—the same black jacket he lent me yesterday. The hood's up over his head, and I can barely see his eyes. Maybe his hood's so low that he can't see me?

Jax sits on the backbench between some boy and Molly. My mind fills with thoughts I don't want. As the bus pulls away,

Molly's voice rises with nonstop chattering at him. What if Jax wants *her* to be his friend instead?

Jax glances up and catches me staring. He quickly ducks his head down and pulls the strings on his hood tighter.

Oh, he saw me, alright! I slump in my seat, my vision blurry. *Fine*. I didn't want to sit by Jax, anyway. I blink back the tears and stare out the window—car after car whips by going in the opposite direction. If only I could hop off this bus and catch a ride back home with one of them. No one would even notice that I didn't show up for the second day of school.

Something pings me on the side of the head. A wad of paper bounces off my hair and lands on the seat next to me. I reach over to brush it away when someone behind me clears their throat. I glance back, and Jax gestures to the paper clump. Reaching over, I unwrap the crumpled wad to see jumbled letters. What does this note even say?

I squint to make out the words *Talk 2 Billy* written in messy handwriting.

Jax can't order me around. I crush the paper and toss it onto the seat.

His note sits there, taunting me. I snatch the wad and uncrumple the paper, smoothing the creases. Then, I fold it four times neatly into a thick rectangle and stick it into my back pocket to discard later.

Now it's like I have a folded rock in my pocket. I can't stop thinking about it. What does Jax mean, *Talk 2 Billy?* How do I go about talking to someone who will probably punch me in the nose?

The image of Billy's mom, Mrs. Simpson, crying on their

oversized white couch with my mom sitting next to her comes into my head. I try to shake the memory away only to be replaced with one of Billy's dad yelling, threatening to send him to his grandma's.

Billy is two rows up, sitting by himself on the bench seat. I can't be sure if he's alone on purpose or if he hates sitting alone. It's hard for me to believe we used to be friends. I wish I understood why everything changed so drastically. I focus on the back of his head and search my brain, trying to remember the last time Billy behaved kindly to me. We were hanging out at his house—the day before he told *everyone* I talked to imaginary friends.

I push the memory of that awful day down and scoot to the edge of my seat. With a quick check in Mr. Jennings's mirror to make sure his eyes are on the road, I move up two rows and plop down in the empty spot next to Billy.

Billy's jaw drops, and he scrambles against the window.

I shift my feet and turn to him. My lips warble as I attempt a smile.

He growls. "What are you looking at?"

"You." The corners of my eyes twitch. I can't keep this up much longer. Now, I'm twitch-winking and warble-smiling at the same time.

Horrified, he mouths the words, "Get away from me."

My hands go numb while my face jitters out of sync with my eyes and mouth. My mind freezes, with no idea how to undo *the situation*. Billy's staring at me, and I'm jittering and twitching. Somehow, my warbling lips stretch open, and the words form. "How you doin'?"

69

He slams his backpack in the space between us. "Buzz off, freak!"

"I was—"

"Quit staring at me!" He plasters himself against the window like he's trying to melt into the bus.

"B-but, I was—"

"Don't you hear me?" he hollers loud enough to rise over the bus chatter. "Go! Away!"

Everyone stops talking. I scramble back to my old seat and slink down. Nope. Never doing that again. Ever.

Mr. Jennings bellows from the front of the bus. "Sit down! Anyone switching seats again will go straight to Principal Wolf's office."

I slide down and pull my backpack tight into my lap. Great. One day of knowing Jax and I've become a liar, a stalker, and a bus seat jumper.

Before Mr. Jennings opens the door at school, he tells me to wait until everyone else gets off the bus. A collective "ooh" sounds. I squeeze my eyes shut and wait until the last kid hops off. Then, I shuffle to the front.

"Meredith, is something wrong?" He smells like Grams—peppermint and eucalyptus, but with a hint of old newspaper.

"No," I mumble, keeping my head low and pressing my hand into my stomach. Something about his concern makes me want to spill my guts, but I can't.

"I'll let it go this time. Next time, I'll have to report you. For your safety." He gives me a kind smile, much different from his proud smile, like the one in the town paper when he received the perfect safety record award. My shoulders drop. Mr. Jennings works so hard to be safe, and I could have messed everything up for him. And for what, Billy? Jax?

I run off the bus and head straight to the computer lab. In fifth grade, we're allowed thirty-minute computer access before homeroom. I need the internet to find a way to break the jinx without having to be friends with Billy.

Inside the computer lab, all stations are open, probably because I'm the only kid who doesn't have a phone. I log in and type the word "jinx" into the search bar. One site claims they can teach you how to make a jinx, which is the opposite of what I want. I click through some other sites, and my fingers cramp. I'm about to give up when a reading goal reminder pops up on the screen telling me to log in how many pages I read yesterday. I hover over the book with googly eyes, debating if I should click it.

The googly eyes disappear, and the words, *Floggy's Cures for a Jinx*, appear on the book's cover.

Floggy? I click on it. Instead of going to my reading chart for this semester, I'm directed to a website. The screen fills with pictures of big noses and red noses, all signs of a jinx. Whoever this Floggy is, they know their stuff. Good news—according to the site's information page, all one needs to break a jinx is to simply do that jinx-blocker in reverse. Bad news—we'd need the original jinxer. Jax was right.

Still, there must be another way. I log off and head to class.

When I get there, Billy's in the hallway leaning against the door, holding it open for me to enter. I bet he plans to slam the door in my face. My feet stop—Billy gestures for me to enter.

Here goes nothing. I tuck my rear and rush past him, but

the door doesn't slam. I must've been too quick.

"Thanks," I say over my shoulder.

"Whatever," Billy mumbles back. He takes his assigned seat across the aisle and behind me.

Each agonizing minute of class passes, and I wait for something to fly into my hair. I dare a peek over my shoulder—Billy's folding sheets of paper into tight triangles. Perfect paper footballs.

My palms sweat, and I rub them against my jeans. No doubt those footballs are meant for my head.

The lunch bell rings. I stack my papers and stow them in the cubby under my desk. Before I can escape from my seat, Billy shuffles behind me. I stiffen and cover my hair, ready for whatever he's planned.

Instead, he scatters the paper footballs across my desk. "For you." Without a glance back, he walks out of the classroom.

Footballs? Why would he give me footballs? Wait. What if they're notes? I unfold the first one carefully, in case he tucked gum or something worse inside.

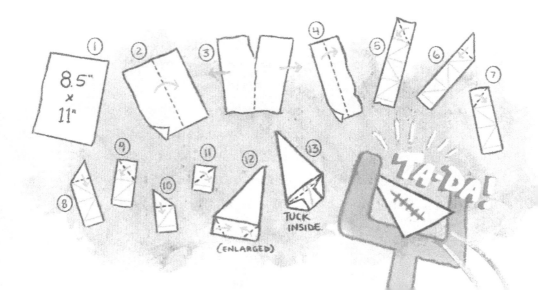

TUCK INSIDE.

(ENLARGED)

TA-DA!

9

TRUTH AND KETCHUP

Today's fish stick day, and the whole cafeteria stinks of an ocean aquarium.

In third grade, our class took a field trip to the aquarium. Afterward, they served fish sticks. There is something unsettling about spending hours learning how to keep the oceans clean and then eating what we're supposed to be saving.

I hold my breath so that my nose hairs don't get saturated with the stench. Whenever they serve fish, that disgusting smell gets stuck in my nose, and I can't ever seem to blow it out for the rest of the day.

I count the seconds and search for Jax. There he is, in the same seat as yesterday. What if Jax still doesn't want to sit with me? My heart sputters, making me cough and waste a perfect inhale in under nine seconds.

My feet refuse to cooperate, but I drag them along and weave through the tables until I'm finally standing across from him—Jax nods to my empty seat.

First thing, I pull out all the unfolded footballs and dump them on the table. "Billy gave me these."

Jax picks one up and examines it. "He gave you paper?"

I slide into my seat and pull out my lunch bag. "They were footballs. But I unfolded each one and couldn't find anything written." I scrunch my face.

"Weird." He eyeballs the rest of the rectangles, dunking fish stick after fish stick into a mound of ketchup before shoving them into his mouth. It's not Heinz, but at least he's ketchup safe.

Most people don't know the truth about ketchup—it's the perfect food—loaded with vitamins and electrolytes. The best part of ketchup is actually the second ingredient—distilled vinegar—a natural, non-toxic germ killer.

But Jax doesn't seem to care about germs or taste. He crunches another bite of the mashed fish stuff covered in an oily, burnt-batter covering. He holds out a stick.

"No." I shake my head and cover my mouth.

"Suit yourself." He pops the fish stick in his mouth and wipes his hands on a napkin. He grabs another one of the papers. "When did he give you these anyway?"

"At the end of class," I tell him. "I bet he wanted to get me in trouble. We're not allowed to have paper footballs."

My throat burns from the greasy fish smell, so I let my vision fall out of focus and go fuzzy to distract me. Now, Jax looks like a static television blob. I unfold my paper bag, put my peanut butter and jelly sandwich on a napkin, and then set out the chips and pear. My vision sharpens when I notice the paper bag is wrinkled. *Shoot!* Heat spreads up the back of my neck. I try smoothing out the brown paper, but it doesn't soothe the frustration pulsing inside me.

Jax peeks over at me and puts his tray on top of the bag. "There," he says.

My shoulders unclench, and the heat fades. "Anyway, I went to the computer lab to research—" I check around to make sure no one is listening and whisper, "jinxes."

"You did?" His voice squeaks real high. "And?"

"I found a couple of ideas. But you might be right. According to one site, *Floggy's Cures for a Jinx,* whoever created it is the Jinx Master."

"Jinx Master." His grin widens. "Cool."

"So, you're still in?"

"For sure." Jax chomps fry number seven, smacking his greasy lips. "Did you tell Billy about our plan?"

"On the bus?" I cringe. "No. He called me a freak and—"

Billy walks up and stops in front of our table. He looks like he wants to sit down. After an awkward silence, his cheeks redden, and he swipes his arm past my pile of napkins and brushes the football papers to the floor.

Jax gets to his feet. "Hey, watch it."

"Or what?" Billy sneers; his chest puffs. "You gonna throw some other fruit at me?" Without waiting for Jax to respond, Billy grabs my pear and sinks his teeth into it. He storms away to the next table and plops down next to Molly and her "Gaggle Boys."

Jax sighs, picking up the paper scraps. "He always makes everything hard."

"You should have talked to him on the bus."

"No way he'd help me, especially after we got in trouble. Had to be you." Jax folds a paper on its creases and makes it back into a football.

"Well, it didn't work."

Jax furrows his brows for a minute, then nods. "Okay. Next time, we both talk to him."

"Fine."

After Jax's sort-of-apology, our table fills with other kids. They say hi to Jax. Probably kids from his class. Everyone at the table talks to Jax like he's their best friend. I scoot over twice to make room. Some of the kids are wearing big face watches like Jax. Did they get a memo I missed?

For the rest of lunch, Billy pretends to ignore us, but I catch him staring every once in a while. Does he want to come and sit with us? It must be a trick. Sometimes he's polite, like holding the door, and the next minute he's making my life miserable.

With the next grade streaming in, the crowded cafeteria morphs into a tunnel of blended noises. Through the commotion, I overhear Alexa tell Isabel, "Let's go to the park after school."

Holy Monkeys! What if they try and come with us today?

I can't stand the chaos. My palms creep up to my ears, and I start to hum. But I don't want to be left out, so I pretend that whatever they say to each other, they are saying to me, too. My eyes widen for "no," and my head slightly nods for a "yes." I get caught up in their conversations and barely even notice the smell or the noise anymore. Jax flashes me a smile making me feel important somehow. Maybe this friend thing isn't so bad.

The two-minute bell rings, and Jax picks up his tray. "See you after school, Mere."

"Don't forget." I pack up my leftover chips before heading back to class.

10

AWKWARD PENGUINS

At the end of the day, I hop on the bus and sweep down the aisle with plans to sit in the back next to Jax. But kids stare at me. Each step becomes heavier and heavier until I'm practically dragging my feet. There are too many ogling eyes, so I duck into a seat near the middle of the bus.

Jax gets up from the back and joins me. "You ready?"

My stomach lurches, and I scoot over to make more room for him. "I hope so."

Billy boards the bus. He's all smug, slapping high fives to everyone in the front rows. He stops when he sees us. His face crinkles, and he stomps down the aisle to our bench. "So, I guess you finally got a boyfriend, huh, freak?" Billy jabs his thumb at Jax. "I guess he doesn't mind the smell."

From a few seats back, Alexa cackles. What? She told Billy, too?

Past Jax's head, I see Alexa kneeling up in her seat and plugging her nose, mocking me.

No. A burn rises in my throat. I clutch my stomach.

Jax stands and pushes into the aisle, so his chest bumps into Billy. "Don't. Ever. Call her that. Got it?"

Bluuorp! I gag and scramble for my backpack. I need a napkin.

Billy stares at me from behind Jax's shoulder.

My stomach heaves again. *Blu—uorp.*

Billy's face pales under his freckles, making them stand out even more. His eyes bulge, and he cups his hand over his mouth. "Stop it!" He turns away, dry heaving.

Bluuorp! Vomit sludges from the back of my throat into my mouth.

Billy turns, shoulders his way to the front, and slams into a seat. His head disappears below the seatback.

Jax sits back down next to me. "You okay?"

I swallow hard and nod. If I talk, I'll start crying. No one's ever stood up for me before like Jax. I lean against the window, willing the tears to stay inside. But one trickles out. *Traitor!* I brush it away.

"No one heard what he said. Besides, that dude farts. Trust me." His shoulders shake from laughing.

Ewww. Boys are so gross. Though he might be right about the 'no one heard' part. I crumple the vomit napkin and throw it in my backpack. The bus pulls away from the school.

Rambling down the road, I gaze out the window and study Jax's reflection in it.

Is his left ear crooked? I knew someone else with a bent ear. The bagger at the grocery store? I can't remember who. At any rate, a crooked ear looks perfect on Jax.

When we get to Jax's stop, kids file off the bus.

Mr. Jennings doesn't close the door. He looks in the rearview mirror and hollers, "C'mon, Mr. Cooper. This is your stop."

"Not today. I'm getting off at the Brown Street stop."

"Do you have a note?"

"No."

"Then, this is your stop."

Jax says, "Meet me at the park," and hustles down toward the door.

The bus is almost empty, and I'm left alone with Billy and Alexa. *Great.* Even Alexa is wearing an old, big face watch.

I hug my knees into my chest and rock, trying to relax with the street bumps and bus creaks until Mr. Jennings pulls up to my stop. Parents are waiting on the sidewalk for the little kids while the older kids scatter off in groups. I get off last and wait for Mr. Jennings to pull away before sprinting toward the park. I don't want him to ask me why I didn't go in the expected direction, toward home.

The park is busy. Too busy. Four ladies powerwalking pass me on the footpath, all talking over each other. At the bottom of a grassy hill, eight kids from my school stand in a circle, kicking around a couple of Hacky Sacks. Two teenagers throw Frisbees to dogs—who are not on a leash. The benches are crammed with older people eating or feeding birds. I grab a swing in the playground and swing high as I can. A groundskeeper wearing blue coveralls prunes pink roses nearby.

Near the base of the grassy mound, Isabel and Alexa flop down near the beanbag kids and watch me. Why do they have to be here? I want to jump into a sinkhole so they can't see me. Numbness creeps in. But I can't think about them anymore.

Besides, my arms and legs still work, so I swing higher and higher. Maybe I can soar into invisibility if I try hard enough.

All those leg pumps wear me out. I let my feet dangle, and the swing's momentum decreases. Instead of looking back toward the grassy hill, I watch the groundskeeper snip each flower gently, the way my dad does. He stops to take a swig of what I imagine to be iced tea from a plastic jug. I wonder if someone prepares it for him with the right amount of lemon, the way Mrs. Dally did. Does he have any dogs, or perhaps a kid? I asked the Dallys once why they didn't have children. My dad stammered, and Mrs. Dally's eyes teared. But Mr. Dally placed his hand on Dad's shoulder and smiled before kneeling so he could look me in the eye. He said they couldn't have kids because their hearts were waiting for mine.

I sure miss him.

My feet drag on the dirt, and the swing comes to a standstill. I need to come up with a plan.

The groundskeeper adds mulch and then moves to clip the next row. All of a sudden, I got it. *The flowers.* That's it! If we replant Mr. Dally's garden, he'd have to go outside, and the jinx will break. Floggy's website probably doesn't know everything. This could work, and bonus, we wouldn't need Billy.

Where is Jax? I need to tell him about the plan. He should be here by now. I count the swing's chain links to distract me.

A few minutes later, Jax crosses the field in long strides. Alexa and Isabel hop up and wave to him while the others call him over, but he doesn't change course. He gives them a wave and continues toward me. I don't want him to see me alone on a swing. I need to get off this seat and act busy. I press my feet on the ground to make sure they haven't fallen asleep. Still numb. If I try to stand up, I'll fall flat on my face.

Jax breaks into a jog and gets on the swing next to me. "Sorry I took so long."

"It's okay." I wiggle my feet and tap them on the ground. Pins and needles, but at least the sensation is returning to them.

He sways from side to side, then says, "You ready?"

When I stamp my foot down, it feels secure. "Sure." I hop off and grab my backpack and sling it over my shoulders. It feels light today.

"So, I came up with a plan," I tell him as we leave the park. "We don't need Billy to break the jinx. We can break it ourselves. All we need to do is plant Mr. Dally's garden again."

"Do you think that will work?"

"I do. I'm just not sure how to get past the jinx yet. I'm working on it."

"If we can't get on the property, we still need Billy."

"Or else come up with a better plan."

He rubs the back of his neck. "I might have an idea."

"Tell me."

Swallowing hard, he says with less confidence, "I'm not even sure I'm right."

"Right now, we need to try anything."

"Okay. Let's do it. Follow me." Jax takes off.

"Why are we always running?" I hop over a sidewalk crack.

Jax looks back and smirks. "Why not." He slows down and jumps over the cracks with me. We leap by a house overgrown with weeds, and a muddy dog jumps out of nowhere, barking and rattling against the fence. The dog's lips pull away from his sharp teeth in a growl.

Jax grabs my arm. "Go-go-go!" We don't stop until we hit the next street.

"That was close." I put my hands on my knees and bend over, panting.

Jax is out of breath, too. He nudges me with his shoulder, and I bump him back.

All the way to the next block, we swerve on the sidewalk, bumping into each other, our arms stuck to our sides. We're like two awkward penguins waddling down the street. The next thing I know, we're standing in front of Dad's nursery. His store is an old brick building a few blocks from our house and used to be a Bucky's hardware store. Plastered on the front window are colorful photos of seasonal flowers and handwritten notices for bake sales or missing pets. We painted the front door lime green, and Dad put a bell on it. The door sign reads, *Shhh, sleeping flowers.* Dad uses it when he's out making deliveries.

"What are we doing here?" I peek through the front window.

Inside, the flower shop glows orange from the overhead lights. Rows of potted plants fill wooden crates lined up against the walls. My favorite part about coming to work with my dad is pretending to get lost in a jungle.

Jax stares at the neon sign hanging above the front door. *Smart Plants and Flowers.* He frowns. "I thought it would be here."

"What would be here? A plant? My dad has all kinds of plants."

"Doesn't matter." His shoulders droop. He stalks away and plops onto the nearby curb. His head slumps into his hands.

I try to think of something to say. If I don't come up with

something, Jax might go home. I plop down next to him. "We can wait for my dad to come back. Or go somewhere else if you want?"

"Don't want to go somewhere else."

"Neither do I." I nip the edge of a fingernail between my teeth and tear off a nail sliver. What's the worst that could happen if we take a little peek inside?

The neon sign blinks like a secret wink for me.

Here goes everything.

I whisper, "Please. Sorry. Thanks." Hoping the magic words I knew when I was little would still work to unlock my secret world.

The faint, lemony scent of daffodil seeps through the glass door frame aimed toward us, like a fog. I take a deep sniff, almost tasting the smell. I imagine running through a field of lemongrass with tall blades of grass whipping around me. I push my way into a clearing and hear a high-pitched voice whispering from inside the store.

"Annabelle, what have you and Floss done?"

A girly voice chimes in. "Hush now! We had to. Can't you see she still needs us?"

I lean in to listen and—*pop!*—the light coming from the neon sign extends and snaps like a rubber band, the same way the lamppost had. Its letters scramble and dance across the sign. When they stop, it reads *Dandy-lion Plants and Flowers*.

Jax jumps from the curb and rushes to the window. "I *knew* it was still here!"

"What? My dad's shop?" I stand to join him, acting cool, just in case, pretending my dad's sign is all I see. I'm used to this sort of stuff happening, but Jax isn't. Plus, I'm not sure what will happen if we do go inside. I haven't been in there for a long time.

"It's not your dad's shop anymore." Jax points to the sign. The letters flicker and spark, teasing me by flashing the word *Dandy-lion* over and over.

Does he see my sign? Well, he did call me Dandy. He also saw the fireflies in the lamp post, so, maybe?

"Let's go inside," I say, not wanting to think about anything other than us having fun together. But if Floss shows up, I'm out of here.

"How do we get in?" Jax cups his hands over his eyes and presses them against the front window.

Before I can explain, something buzzes to the window and peeks out. It must notice me too because its eyes widen. A hummingbird? Hard to tell. I lean in to get a closer view, and the bird whizzes away.

"This way," I say and lead him to the front door. The ting-a-ling of a bell hanging overhead announces our entrance, and with a sweeping bow, I hold the door open. I've done this before when I've brought kids here. All they saw was my dad's shop.

"Now, imagine. We're in a flower shop like my dad's. But instead, it's magical. And it belongs to me. It's my shop."

11

Hummingbird With A Top Hat

One hop over the threshold and I'm inside the Dandy-lion shop. I wave Jax inside. "All clear."

Jax steps wide over the threshold, his eyes big as black cat petunias. "Wow."

"It's all pretend. But still." I close the door and turn to see if Jax's faking. Not paying attention, I walk through a cobweb. Stale plant pollen releases into the air. *A-choo.* "Pickles!" I struggle to hold back the next sneeze. "Pickles, pickles!" *A-a-choo. A-a-choo.*

There never used to be dust in here. How long has it been?

Jax heads straight, checking from ceiling to floor. His mouth flaps open like a hungry guppy. He turns left at the chrysanthemums.

"Don't get lost," I call after him.

The shop appears small from the outside, but that's only the front space. There's a giant warehouse in the back.

In the middle of the front room, old receipts and seed packets clutter the retail countertop where Dad rings up the plants. The Dandy-lion's a copycat store that's set up identical to Dad's shop. Bookshelves surround the reading space next to the front door.

Dad believes you can't properly grow plants if you don't read to them, so he keeps loads of books in the shop. He also sells tea. A few times a year, he makes limited batches using edible flowers in the shop. We sell out every time, especially the honeysuckle and lemon flavors. Customers sip tea and read to the plant display while sitting on the benches dad built for the shop. New customers might think it's strange, but his regulars love it. Mr. Jennings, the bus driver, comes in on most Saturdays. That's how he knows me.

I poke around the flower pots looking for the hummingbird I saw from outside. No sign of anything with wings, but I swear a daffodil giggled. I glance at the yellow flower, and its six petals fold in on its trumpet center like it's hiding a smile.

I tear my attention away and holler to the room, "Hello?"

My echo responds, *Hello?*

No one answers, so I give up finding the hummingbird and check out the front desk glass case. Inside are tea concoctions wrapped in homemade bags, each stamped with *Dandy-lion* next to the type of tea. No sign of honeysuckle or lemon, but there's a batch of rosehip. As a little kid, I refused to drink tea with weird names, especially if the word "hip" was involved. I thought there were real bones mixed in with leaves. But when I was eight, I helped Dad make a batch. Turns out *hip* is the rose's fruit. The flavor tastes sweet and tart, like green apples.

When I open the glass case, a perfume of roses is released.

Quick, I close the latch and take a whiff of orange rinds to fill my sinus.

A tissue box appears next to the old metal cash register on top of the glass countertop. Two big jumps, and I pluck out a tissue barely in time to sneeze. *Ah-choo*. I toss the tissue in the wastebasket and stare at the register.

I run my fingers over the brass keys and notice a picture on the wall. It's a framed photo of me, my parents, and Grams at the lake when I was five or six. I pull it off the wall to get a closer look. It's the same picture from Dad's shop, except the hummingbird from the window is flitting behind us in this photograph. I shake the frame trying to make the bird fall out. Instead, it flutters its wings against the glass.

I drop the picture face-up on the counter and hop back. "Woah!"

"What's wrong?" Jax yells from one of the rows.

"Ummm. Nothing." I clasp my hands together so tight my fingers strangle to red. An odd memory tingles like déjà vu. This new Dandy-lion is much different from the shop where I used to play.

Taking a step and leaning forward to study the photo, the bird in the picture looks friendly enough, like a hummingbird fairy, but not. Underneath its long hummingbird beak hangs a grey handlebar mustache, and below is a big, cheesy smile. I can't remember if hummingbirds are supposed to have mouths. I grab the frame and brace myself, expecting a shock. My hands don't feel any different.

I carry the picture over to Jax, who I find wandering through the big pots. I point to the bird-thing. "Can you see this thing floating behind my family and me in this picture?"

Jax looks at the photo and sighs. "I keep telling you. I see what you see."

Right—fireflies and grinning hummingbirds with mustaches. But not once did Jax mention the smiling flowers. He can't really see anything. He's merely good at pretending. Whatever. Hopefully, he's better at breaking jinxes than he is going along with what I say.

Soon as I hang the picture back up, the same bird-thing whizzes past and lands on the daffodil. I reach out to touch it but pull my hand away. This is no ordinary hummingbird. I mean, it has the same shimmery wings of a hummingbird, but with the body of a teeny-tiny fairy-person complete with arms and legs—wearing a tuxedo.

The bird taps a black top hat firmly upon its tiny head, nods at Jax, and flutters a wing my way as if to say, "Get a load of this, girl."

But then it speaks in a little guy's high-pitched voice. "What's wrong with her?" It sounds like when you suck the air out of a helium balloon.

"There you are." Jax brightens up and rushes over. "Not sure what's wrong with her. Sorry, Mr. M., she can't remember anything. But I'm sure glad to see you."

He sees the bird thing? Not sees him, but *knows* him!

"How can you see—" I clamp my mouth shut. I'm not sure I want to know the answer.

Mr. M. leans against the daffodil stem with his legs crossed, picking at his teeth with a blackberry thorn. "Ahhh, how unfortunate. Sorry, Jax, you need to let her work it out on her own."

"I figured." Jax rubs his forehead.

"Have no fear. It will all come back to her."

What will come back to me? *And hello!* I'm right here.

I squat and get on this tiny guy's level. He's not wearing an actual tuxedo; black and white feathers on his body create a pattern that resembles a tuxedo. And his cummerbund is nothing more than an iridescent sash tied around his waist. A name tag on his feathery white chest reads MR. MILKE.

Mr. Milke blinks behind thick, silver-rimmed glasses. "Hello," he says in his helium voice.

I want to answer, but I can't. I gawk at his rainbow wings of shimmering feathers as if, somehow, that's the only thing odd about him. Can something glittering be dangerous? His sharp beak makes me think so.

"How can I help you?" He tips his head to one side.

"Help *me*?" I ask.

Jax's head swivels between the two of us. Then he leans down to talk to him. "How ya been, Mr. M.?"

"Good. Good." Mr. Milke removes his top hat and smooths his feathery head before plopping it back on. "It's been a while. Where you been hiding out?"

"Oh, you know, here and there." Jax is acting all calm, not weird at all, as if talking to a hummingbird with a top hat is the most normal thing in the world.

"Your mom doing okay?"

Jax pauses, then runs his hand through his hair and massages the back of his neck. "Best she can, I guess."

Should I ask if something's wrong with his mom?

"Sometimes, that's all we can do." Mr. Milke gives Jax that look adults do when they know something you don't.

Jax picks at his cuticles, and the room grows quiet until he finally speaks. "Mr. M., I hate to ask, but can you help us out? We need one of your potions."

Mr. Milke stuffs his wing-hands into the side pockets of his sash. "What for?"

Jax whispers something.

"I'm sorry, Jax. I can't. You know the drill."

Jax nods and looks at the ground. "I understand."

Can't what? My eyes dart back and forth between the two of them until Jax clears his throat and says, "Well, we'll need the potion for Billy Simpson then. We're working on a hard case."

"Billy Simpson, huh?" Mr. Milke's voice trills with cheerfulness.

"Yep." Jax grins.

"Okey-dokey."

In a blink, Mr. Milke glides around the room, whistling a tune familiar to me. He plucks a bluebell flower bulb and stitches the petals together with a saffron thread. Flitting from flower to flower, he puts a wisp of rosemary leaf, a sprinkle of lavender, and a dab of honeysuckle nectar into the drawstring bluebell. Finally, he lands on a white lily petal and lifts his glasses to scrutinize me. "I've seen her like this before, Jax. People get inside her head, and she forgets who she is."

"What people?" I ask.

"The ones who don't understand what you can see," Mr. Milke answers.

So—everyone.

I reach out to touch the drawstring bluebell, wishing I could stay here with Jax, talking to a wise hummingbird all day, like I used to with the flowers, the fireflies and—

"Wait! I remember you!" I sidestep and stumble into a fern plant. Jax catches me before I hit the ground.

Mr. Milke swoops up to my face. "She okay?" The little guy sounds worried.

"She's fine." Jax steadies me before letting go of my arm.

A million prickles tingle the spot on my arm where he caught me, not to mention my heart rate speeds up and makes a nosedive for my stomach. I must be in a dream if Jax knows Mr. Milke too. That's the answer, and I need to wake up. I pinch my arm. "Ouch!" Nothing's changed, still in the flower shop—except now, Jax is smiling.

"You're awake, Miss Dandy." Mr. Milke's high-pitched voice squeaks in my ear. "Don't let anyone tell you otherwise, not even you."

This is all wrong. My heart pounds. I back away from them and search for an exit.

"I think she figured it out," Jax says.

Mr. Milke sweeps over to the daffodil and says, "Annabelle, I told you this was a bad idea."

The daffodil wilts; its trumpet-shaped petals purse into a

pout. "I'm sorry," she says softly.

Jax rushes to the daffodil with a frown. "No, don't be sad. She's fine." His eyes are full of concern when he looks back at me. "Tell them you're okay, Mere. Please."

But I'm not fine. Everything is not okay. This was supposed to be *my* world. *My* Fancies. But, Jax knows them. I swallow hard. "I—I gotta go." I back toward the door, my eyes glued to them. "Grams is calling me." A lie.

Mr. Milke perks up. "Do give Grams my best. Tell her to visit soon. We miss her."

"Uh, sure." I fumble for the door handle.

Jax points at me. "She's lying."

Mr. Milke frowns. "Now, now, lying's never good. Isn't that right, Miss Dandy?"

"I'm sorry. I didn't mean to." I let my hand fall from the doorknob. Now I've disappointed a daffodil, Jax, and a talking bird. I'm not sure why this bothers me, but it does.

Mr. Milke crosses his little wings. "And I accept your apology. Be mindful of telling fibs. I know a boy who told so many lies he can't close his mouth anymore. Lies spill right off his tongue." He tips his hat.

I should show more remorse, but all I can picture is a kid with a cherry fruit roll dangling from his mouth.

"He's not a kid any longer," Mr. Milke says, answering my thoughts, and it freaks me out. If he can read my mind, who knows what else he might find out? I hum loud in my head and struggle not to think of anything else.

Mr. Milke doesn't seem concerned. He draws the saffron string closed and holds out the cinched bluebell bag. It's no bigger than a thimble. I stop humming. My gut tells me to take it, but I have no clue why. He shakes it at me, waiting. I open my hand and extend it to him, and he drops the tiny sack into my palm.

"What do I do with this?"

"Tie it on your necklace. You need to keep it close by." He glides back to the daffodil and lands beside her. "You'll know when it's time."

"Sure. Okay." I unclasp my necklace and loop the bag's string through my silver chain.

"One more thing." Mr. Milke plucks a tiny dandelion flower from the ground beside the daffodil. In the time it takes him to swoop to me, the yellow flower matures into a seed head. He holds it out in front of my face. "Make a wish."

I shake my head. "The seeds will go everywhere and ruin the other plants."

Mr. Milke frowns and tucks it under his top hat. "Perhaps another time."

Jax sticks out his pinkie finger to shake Mr. Milke's little hand. "I appreciate your help. Tell everyone I said 'hi.'"

"Will do. Oh, and Jax, be patient with your mom. Everyone needs time to adjust to new things." He bobs his head toward me and whizzes away in a blur.

Jax walks over to me at the door. "Ready?"

"So, what do we do now?"

"We still need Billy's help. Mr. M. made that potion for Billy."

I about jump out of my skin. "What? No. First, you trick me into bringing you here, and now you want me to give the bulliest bully in town a magic potion?"

Jax's forehead puckers. "We can't break the jinx without Billy. Anyway, we don't have to *give* him the potion. We'll use it to convince him to help us."

My hand wraps around the bluebell, and I'm ready to yank it off and tell Jax I'm done. Then I remember Mr. Dally still needs our help, and my tongue sticks to the roof of my mouth. As much as I want to unjinx him, all I can imagine is Billy striking me with his paper footballs.

There's only one thing to do, and I do it. I bolt out the door.

12

HALF NOD AND
A PROMISE

As soon as I'm outside, I flee, wanting to get as far away from my dad's flower shop as possible.

"Meredith, wait up!" Jax yells.

"No! Leave me alone. My dad knows the Chief of Police. And the FBI." I'm so nervous, I spout off lie after lie. "He's a secret agent in the CIA. They have eyes everywhere, you know."

Jax catches up. He barely broke a sweat. "What are you doing?"

I skid to a stop and almost knock myself over before running the other way. I have no idea what I'm doing. I mean, I do lots of weird things when I'm nervous. I guess escaping my imagination makes me downright scared. Huffing and puffing, I zigzag back and forth across the sidewalk.

"Your house is the other way," he calls from behind me.

Darn it! He's right. My shoelace comes untied and slaps on the pavement. Now I'm struggling not to trip over the laces, zigzagging back and forth, and jumping wildflowers sprouting from the sidewalk cracks—all at the same time.

Holy monkeys! Billy's right. I am a freak.

But I can't stop. Block after block—I'm panting harder and harder. Next thing I know, I'm smack-dab in the middle of the sidewalk in front of the Dally's house. How did I get here? I quickly cover my left eye and gasp out, "Not me, not me, not me," and run back to Jax.

I scream, "Why did you do that?"

He stiffens. "Do what?"

"You made me do the jinx! I stepped onto their sidewalk without protection!"

"Why're you mad? You showed *me* how."

"But I didn't want to." I hang my head and tromp away in the direction of my house. "Leave me alone," I say, crossing the street.

He follows me anyway.

"Stop it."

He matches my pace.

I slam on the brakes. "Why are you doing this to me? I don't even understand how you can see any of this!"

"I don't know. I swear. But I've tried to explain it before. We were friends. Back when—"

"Stop! You're just making fun of me." I cross my arms. "Forget it. I'm done."

"I won't tell anyone you see them." Jax pushes his hair out of his eyes. "We need to use the potion, and that's all."

"I can't!" That's the problem. He'll never understand what it's like to be me. I can't rely on Fancies for help or to be my friends. They go away whenever they want and leave me here, stuck all by myself.

"Mere, listen—"

"No. You listen—" The streetlights illuminate. "Great. Now, I'm late. Because of *you*. And I'll be grounded for life." I'll be grey-haired and thirty, sitting in my room and still trying to explain to my parents that Jax tricked me.

"But I had to show you."

"It's a trick. The whole thing's a trick. And even if it were true, you could have asked Mr. Milke for anything. You could've asked him to break the jinx. But instead, you wanted him to help Billy."

"You don't understand."

"I don't want to." I stamp my foot on the ground. "You're selfish. You don't care about anyone else. You only do what you want."

Jax's crooked ear reddens, and he glares at me for what seems like forever. "That's it! I'm done! I don't need you, anyway." He throws his arms up and storms across the street. "I'm finished with you. I'm finished with everybody."

I fiddle with the flower bag attached to my necklace. "Wait, don't you need this?"

He spins back at me. "For what! Only *you* can use the potion." He kicks a rock.

All I can see is him walking away. I want to follow him, but I can't. Instead, I sprint as fast as I can until I make it to the edge of my driveway.

The house is all lit. I'm surprised there's not a line of police cars with search and rescue dogs. Every step I take makes my stomach clench even tighter. My belly starts to hurt so bad that I want to curl over. Soon as I swing open the front door, the loud conversation inside the living room ceases. Everyone stares at me as I trudge my way inside.

Mom wobbles to a stand. "Meredith, where have you been?"

Dad rushes past her to hug me. Behind him, Grams crosses her arms and taps her foot.

"I went t-to the park. I couldn't see the streetlights." My stomach heaves. I need to stop lying. I suck on my tongue to keep it from rolling out of my mouth. It feels numb, but not any longer. "I'm sorry."

Dad steps back and throws his hands up. "Someone could have kidnapped you."

"I would have called if I had a phone," I tell him. I'm already in trouble, might as well ask for a phone.

"What were you doing at the park?" Mom fires off question after question without pause. "Were you alone? Were there any other kids there? Adults?"

I hold up my hand for a turn to talk and force myself to remain calm. "Dad said I could go. And Isabel and Alexa were at the park."

"Humph." Grams plants her hands on her hips.

Mom cocks an eyebrow. "Isabel Herrera?"

"Yes."

Her lashes flutter. "Well, at least you were with friends."

I don't answer. Not answering isn't the same as lying.

Dad's not so persuaded. "I don't care if she did hang out with friends. It's late. Anything could have happened to her."

Mom snaps at him, "Phillip, we'll talk about it later. You remember what Dr. Richter said about Meredith finding friends."

And there she was, back to talking about me like I'm not here.

"Darn right, we'll talk about it later," Dad grumbles. "To the dinner table, young lady."

I follow them to the kitchen and sit down to cold turkey and broccoli. I detest the weirdness of broccoli in my mouth, like chomping on tree stalks with mushy leaves, but there's no way I'm complaining. I take a small bite off the bushy top and discreetly spit it into my napkin. No one notices except Grams, who spends the whole meal staring sideways at me.

I wait for her to bring up Jax, but she clams up for the rest of the meal.

After dinner, I crawl into bed under cool sheets. Soon as they've warmed up from body heat, I hear a soft knock on the door.

"Come in."

Grams peeks in, scanning the room like she's searching for intruders. Satisfied, she shuffles in wearing heeled slippers and sits next to me. The corner of her mouth twitches, and I know she's on to me when she pulls a tissue from her pocket. "Hard day, huh?"

I blow my nose, too exhausted to even say "exactly."

Grams reaches for the extra pillow at the bottom of the bed. Fluffing it out, she slips the cushion under my head. "This isn't like you to make us worry. You know you scared us half to death, right?"

I nod.

She cups my warm cheeks between her cold hands. "Do you want to tell me what you were doing out so late tonight?"

Don't cry. I swallow and shake my head.

She sighs and gently smooths my hair back. "Did you meet with Jax today?"

My head nods, like all I can do is a nod and shake.

She whispers, "Are there any other new friends you want to discuss?"

"No." I can't bear to tell her.

"Come with me." She eases my blankets back and takes my hand. "To the window." She pulls the curtains open and stares out at the night sky. "What do you see?"

"It's dark," I say. Is this a trick?

"Yes, dark. What else?"

"Nothing." But the fireflies hovering inside the light post globe protest with glowing swirls. I ignore the one waving at me. My heart somersaults. I've never lied to her before.

Grams' face falls. "This is a challenging time for you, I know. You're almost eleven, and there's a lot to learn. I want you to be careful while you figure out yourself. Will you try to do that for me?"

"Yes." But I don't dare ask what she means by figuring out myself. That could lead to an hour-long conversation.

"Good. And no more lying, hmm?" Grams gives me her trusting smile.

I start to say, "never again." Instead, I half-nod and promise to try. "Grams, can I ask you a question?"

"Anything."

"How come making friends is so hard?"

"I don't know." She sighs. "Probably because deep down, we're never sure if we're doing it right."

"Everyone else is doing it right."

"Oh, you think so?" Grams chuckles. "Every single one of those kids who has friends today worries they might not have them tomorrow. Sometimes, they're even right."

"Then, why even try?" My voice cracks, and tears well up.

She fishes another tissue from her pocket and holds it out. "Because true friendship can last forever. The trick is you must work at it. You also should be willing to accept your friends for everything they are. You can't just take the good. Sometimes the bad, or the different, is what makes someone special."

I frown. My different doesn't make me special. Maybe my bad is too bad. "Did you have a best friend at my age?" I try to picture her at almost eleven. It's impossible.

"Yes. And my friend's different, that's for sure." She laughs, then stares off like she's looking at something very far away. "Okay, off to bed."

She tucks me in and leans over to give me a forehead kiss. "If you ever want to talk about *anything,* know I am always here for you."

I burrow under the blankets and yawn.

Grams goes to close the curtains but stops halfway. "Sweet dreams." She shuts off the bedside light and blows me a kiss from the doorway. A moment later, she's humming away down the hall.

Once I'm certain she's gone, I roll on my side to stare out the window. Outside the glass panes, stars sparkle, lighting up the sky like a Christmas tree. They remind me of the "Twinkle, Twinkle" song Grams used to sing to me. Tonight, some of the stars appear orange, or purple, or blue. It's hard to pick out a single color because they keep changing. Usually, this kind of thing bothers me, but stars don't have to hide what they are. I'm the only one who can't be me.

13

NOT A BILLY THING

In the Midwest, maple tree leaves change to red, and leaves on the green ash brighten to yellow. I jump over a palm-size maple leaf floating in a puddle. There's a damp mustiness, stale, almost sweet, as the leaves decay.

Nothing lasts forever.

I swing my backpack onto the bus seat. Some of the girls in the back talk about a party this past weekend. They're all wearing matching hair ties on their wrist. Glittery ones that are pretty.

It doesn't matter. I don't have time for a hair tie.

Mr. Dally is still trapped. It's been six weeks, and nothing's changed. Except Jax sits at another table with his classmates at lunch, and I sit at our table alone. There must be a way to save Mr. Dally and keep the Fancies out of the plan. I've been thinking about it, and I need to talk with Jax. Even if he isn't my friend, he might agree to help again, this one time.

Mr. Jennings opens the bus door at Jax's stop. My hands go sweaty, and I wait for him to board. But he doesn't get on the bus.

At school, I search everywhere for Jax but can't find him. Something tells me Jax isn't coming. He's gone forever, probably packed up and moved far away. So he doesn't have to see me again.

By lunchtime, I'm desperate to get out of my seat.

"Twelve, eleven, ten," I count the clock ticking down to the bell. Kids watch me, but I don't care; they didn't lose their only friend. They have millions of them. "Three, two, one!" I yell.

"Meredith, enough," Ms. Reeder says from her desk. The lunch bell rings.

"I'm sorry," I tell her and pack my stuff, rushing to the girls' bathroom and slamming myself into a toilet stall. I unravel a whole roll of toilet paper and dab my eyes to stop tears. I wash my face in the sink and sulk to the cafeteria. My nose is snotty and stuffy, and I can't smell a thing. I end up at our usual table—it's empty. No one sits with me. They would have if Jax were here.

Searching inside my lunch bag, I remember my sandwich sitting on the counter. My stomach doesn't even complain. I'm about to leave when I hear someone shuffle to the table. I peer up, hoping to see Jax.

It's Billy. He drops his tray on the table and sits down across from me. I want to bolt, but I can't, so I hold my breath to slow my heart rate. It's a trick I learned on one of those wild animal shows. I once watched a man play dead for an hour to keep a lion from eating him.

Boom, boom, boom. My heart pounds.

Can Billy hear heartbeats? I want mine to say, *Not me, not me, not me.*

Cautiously, I put one foot on the bench and keep my sight

on him. His eyes narrow. We're locked in some strange staring contest. In my head, I can hear the deep-voiced man who talks over the wild animals in the show.

"On the plains of the Serengeti, one will survive. The wild beast stares down his prey." Just when the narrator is about to describe my death scene, Billy asks, "Where's your lunch?"

"I forgot it," I mumble. Nothing's going right today.

Billy's head pivots around like he's making sure no one's watching, then he takes a chocolate chip cookie off his tray and puts it on a napkin. He slides it across the table in front of me.

Is he trying to trick me?

His face squints like he's fighting a sneeze. Copper freckles bunch together at the corners of his mouth, and he kind of smiles.

I don't want to eat a cookie that Billy's hand touched, but not accepting it seems risky.

Here goes nothing. I pick the cookie up by the edge and take a small bite. "Yum." I place the rest back onto the napkin.

I'm not sure what to do next, so I laugh, wishing my laugh came out soft, like other girls. It's not. Mine's more of an angry goose honk.

Without warning, my nose itches, "Pickles!" But I can't stop the sneezing. *Ah-choo, ah- ah-choo.*

Billy slinks a few seats down to the corner, sliding his lunch tray with him.

Once my sneezing fit ends, he whispers across the table, "You know Molly? She lives next door to your friend Junior's house—"

"Junior? You mean Jax?"

"Keep it down." Billy swivels his head right and left. "Yeah, him. Well, Molly's mom got a call this morning and went right over to Jax's house after." He takes a hunk full of meat and stuffs it into his mouth. A trickle of brown gravy seeps out a corner of his lip. "Molly's dad had to drive her to school."

Don't gag. Don't gag. I grab the napkin from under the cookie and hold it over my mouth.

"What happened?" I ask.

He shrugs. "Something about his mom. She sick?"

Is she sick? Or maybe Jax is. I jump up from the table, almost tripping over the bench. I rush to the principal's office and throw open the door. Billy almost bumps into me when he charges in next.

Mrs. Lizard-Face is talking on the phone. She ignores us as she smacks her thin lips and chats about a vacation she's taking to Florida. For a brief second, I want to remind her to wear sunscreen. But then I want to scream at her to get off the phone.

Billy drums his fingers on the counter and hums loudly.

She glares at both of us like we're bothersome flies she wants to slurp up. Her thick glasses lock onto his fingers, and she hangs up. "Can I help you?" she croaks at Billy.

Billy lifts his hand and hovers it over the silver bell, ready to *ting, ting, ting* it and get us both in trouble.

I blurt, "I'm here for Jax Cooper."

Mrs. Lizard-Face turns her attention to me. "Do I look like his secretary to you?"

"No, but we can't find him. We think maybe he's sick?"

She sighs. "I see." She taps her fake long fingernails across a keyboard. "And you are?"

"Meredith. Meredith Smart."

The door to the principal's office opens. "One moment, Miss

Smart." Mrs. Lizard-Face points her chin at Billy and yanks her head toward the open door. "*You* can go in now."

"Why?" Billy asks.

"To see Principal Wolf." She glances at her screen. "Who made the referral this time?"

Principal Wolf appears in her doorway, looking first to Lizard then to Billy. His face reddens, and I know he's a volcano ready to explode.

"No, he's here with me," I quickly say. "He didn't do anything. We're *both* checking on Jax."

Mrs. Lizard-Face turns to Principal Wolf. "Never mind that message. I'll handle this." After the principal goes back inside her office, Lizard's eyes flick back and forth between Billy and me. "Interesting," she murmurs. "Well, Ms. Smart, I am not at liberty to give out personal information. I suggest you call your friend after school."

"But I don't have his number."

"What a shame."
She rifles through a stack
of papers on her desk.

I motion to Billy that we should go and head towards the door. "Oh, Ms. Smart?"

I pivot around.

She gets up from her desk and offers me a flyer. "Don't forget to ask your parents about coming to the autumn fest." Her long nail taps the corner of the page where a phone number had been written in black pen.

My heart flips. I want to thank her, but she reaches back and answers the phone before I have the chance.

After we leave the office, I turn to Billy. "You have a phone, right?"

He takes it out of his pocket. When he tries to hand it to me, I freeze. I know how to use a phone, but this one has more buttons than our television remote.

Billy's lips creep into a half-smile. "Here, let me." He dials the number from the flyer and gives the phone to me. It rings and rings and rings.

I shake my head and give him the phone.

He presses the END key and puts his phone away. "What now?"

I lean against the wall. "I don't know."

"You could ditch and go find him?" His face gleams with mischief.

"I don't know where he lives."

He furrows his brow. "Dude, he's your friend, and you don't even know where he lives?"

"I'm not a dude," I remind him. Sheesh.

"Wait here." Billy heads back into the office. A few minutes later, he returns with a scrap of paper. "Here. Got it."

I give him points for getting the address, but that still doesn't mean I can ditch school. "Would you go with me? I mean, just to Jax's house." I can't believe I'm asking Billy for help. "And after school," I quickly add. "Not now."

"Why would I do that?"

My mind fumbles for a reason. "I don't know."

Billy holds the address out to me like he wants me to take it so he can be done with me. But then he glances at the paper in his hand and shoves it into his pocket. "Fine. Meet me at the gym after school."

The bell rings, and I sprint to the empty gym.

Billy's already there standing by the exit on the far side of the gym. He scans inside left and right, like he's done this before, and waves me over. "Stay low until we're off the school grounds." He pushes open the exit door that only faculty are permitted to use.

I peer out to the side parking lot. No parent pick-up or busses here. "Why can't we go out the front entrance?"

"My dad's waiting for me there. We're going to have to go around the other side of the school to leave."

When I don't answer, Billy says, "I don't have all day. You want to see Jax or not?"

I do, more than anything. Deep breath—I duck out the door and stay low until we make our way past the school. Billy doesn't say anything as we move from street to street. I want to ask if we should pretend we're trees, but I don't think it's a Billy kind of thing. My stomach churns into a knot.

A few blocks later, Billy stops in front of a single-story, wood-trimmed house. He checks the paper. "This is it."

I'm not sure what I expected, but not this. His house is painted soft blue with yellow trim. There's a flower box under each windowsill filled with pansies and asters, even sweet alyssum. Their front yard is grass except for a river rock stream running through it. A wooden bridge, wide enough for one person to cross, arcs over the rocks.

Billy and I go up the driveway and walk onto a wooden ramp leading to the front door. There's a doorbell, but I raise my hand to knock instead. I pause. Something tells me not to.

"What are you waiting for?" Billy asks.

I pull my hand back. "Should we be here?"

Billy reaches past me and knocks three times. "Too late."

The door opens. Jax stands there with his hair a mess, but he doesn't look sick. "What are you doing here?" He sounds irritable.

"You didn't come to school today," I answer.

From inside the house, a cheerful, sing-songy voice calls, "Honey, who is it?"

"No one, Mom."

"Well, it has to be someone. No ones don't knock."

A shuffling and then rolling noise gets closer until the door pulls wide open. Jax moves so his mom can wheel out onto the front porch. Sunlight reflects off her metal chair and shines into my eyes. I squint and cover the glare with my hand. When I open them, Jax is scowling at me.

Mrs. Cooper smiles with the whitest teeth I've ever seen.

Jax looks like her, except she's darker and larger, and right now, she's friendly. I feel like I know her, somehow.

"What's the matter, child? Never seen a woman on wheels before?"

Jax squeezes the back of his neck and looks down.

Before I can say anything, Billy asks, "Why are you in a wheelchair?" He doesn't sound mean, but it's not exactly polite.

Mrs. Cooper laughs a happy laugh, and it makes me feel at ease.

"Good question, young man. What's your name?"

"Billy."

"Ah, Billy Simpson. Well, Billy, not everyone has two good legs to walk."

He nods as if satisfied with her answer.

She glances down the street. "Is school out already?"

"Yes," Billy says.

"Well then, I'll leave you here to talk. It's nice to see you, Billy. It's nice to see you as well, Meredith."

She knows my name?

Mrs. Cooper wheels back inside. Jax follows her inside and starts to close the door.

"Wait." I jam my foot in between the frame. "Are you okay? Why weren't you at school?"

"None of your business! You might want to move your foot." I pull my foot back, and Jax slams the door.

Billy shoots me a look. "I thought you two were friends."

"Me too." Now, what's going to happen to Mr. Dally? Jax didn't seem to care I brought Billy. I check my watch, calculating how long it will take me to get to Dad's shop. Close, but I should make it. "I've gotta go."

"Sure. Whatever." Billy clumps down the porch ramp. "Good luck with your boyfriend."

"He's not my boyfriend."

"Keep telling yourself that." He jumps the last railing. "Oh. And if you tell anyone I helped you, I'll make your life miserable. Got it?"

"Uhhh. Well, thanks for coming with me." But before he disappears, I have to ask. "Billy, do you know a Mr. Milke?"

"No." He runs off.

I guess it's only Jax and me. And now, he doesn't want to be my friend.

14

Juniper Berries

When I arrive at Dad's shop, I glance at the sign. No flickering. No Dandy-lion. The letters read *Smart Plants and Flowers*. Maybe, if I close my eyes tight first, I'll see my sign.

Fingers crossed, I squeeze them shut and pop them wide open.

Nothing. I huff, blowing my bangs up like a wispy cloud. Well, last time, I didn't see the Dandy-lion sign right away. Maybe there's still a chance Mr. Milke's store is inside. I peek through the window. Dad waves me in.

Ting-a-ling-a-ling. I close the door behind me.

"Hey, Mere. What were you doing out there?"

"Nothing." I slink into the reading nook and start pulling books off the shelf to check behind them. Mr. Milke could fit anywhere.

Dad crosses his arms and leans against the counter. "Now, what are you doing?"

"Cleaning." I slide the books back into their slots and dash

over to the counter to check our family picture on the wall. Mr. Milke's not in there either.

"Hmm, that doesn't look like cleaning to me. How about you go water the fresh blooms?"

"Okay." I fill the old metal watering can to the brim and take it to the back room. "Mr. Milke, are you here?" I whisper, pushing aside the leaves and searching. "Please. I need you to help me with Jax."

Kssch! Juniper bushes sway behind me.

Holy Monkeys! Floss's using all his might to swing on the shrub's trailing branches, spilling the juniper berries all over the floor.

"Stop!" I tell him. "You're going to get me in trouble."

"Who are you talking to?" Dad springs up behind me.

Floss scuttles away, leaving me with a mess to clean up. I stand and give Dad my best smile. "The flowers. Don't you want me to talk to them?"

"Sure. The roses are in bloom. Make sure and talk to them, too." He gives me two thumbs up before noticing the berries. "Did you pick those?"

"Yes." I cover for Floss. "Can we make juniper berry tea?"

"Good idea. How about you gather the ripest berries, and we'll pick through them later for the best." He whistles his way to the front.

I glance around. Dad's shop isn't my shop.

Ting-a-ling-a-ling.

"Good afternoon, Dalila!" Dad's cheerful voice carries throughout the store.

Jax's mom? What's she doing here? I creep closer to

listen to them.

"Good day to you," Mrs. Cooper says. "You remember my son?"

"Sure, I do," Dad says. "Hello, Junior. You sure have grown."

Junior?

"I go by Jax now." He sounds all mopey.

Mrs. Copper chuckles. "No one gets away with calling him Junior these days."

"Jax?" Dad pauses. "Ohhh! Well, what do you know? So, you're the infamous Jax. Why didn't you mention you were Dalila's son on the phone the other night?"

I peek around the corner and see his mom wheeling up to the register. Dad catches my eye and waves me over. "Mere, come out and say hello."

My eyes find everything except Mrs. Cooper's face while I skulk out from my hiding place. Is she going to tell Dad I was at her house?

"Hello, Meredith."

"Hello, Mrs. Cooper," I croak out.

Dad wiggles his brows at me and nods his head toward Jax. "Now, we have our mystery solved." He steps from behind the counter. "What can I help you with, Dalila?"

"A few more foxgloves and perhaps a book. I read the last one you suggested to my mums. They're in full bloom."

"Wonderful news. I have some black-eyed Susan's in stock, too, and I know just the book they'll enjoy. Mere, please make Mrs. Cooper a cup of tea." Dad tosses his chin toward the back room, which means "go" in adult.

He turns to Mrs. Cooper. "Orange rind, right?"

"Perfect." She beams a smile at him.

I shamble to the back and turn on the kettle. Waiting for the water to boil, I scoop orange tea out of the canister and into the infuser. When I bring her teacup out on a saucer, Dad's sitting on a bench next to Mrs. Cooper in her wheelchair. Jax leans against the wall with his hands crossed.

"Thank you." Mrs. Cooper takes a sip. "You two kids go visit while I speak to Mr. Smart now, you hear?"

"No," Jax says to my surprise like I've done something wrong. He's the one who slammed the door in my face.

Mrs. Cooper angles her head at Jax. "I didn't say 'would you like to visit' now did I, young man?"

Dad's stern eyes lock with mine, and he jerks his head toward the back room, another sign for "go." But faster.

While Jax drags the soles of his tennis shoes across the floor, Dad stands and pulls a book from the shelf. "This one's perfect. All about medicinal teas." Dad flips to a page and reads in an exaggerated voice about the benefits of orange rind tea on aches and pains.

Once Jax and I make it past the rows of plants, I whip around. "Why are you mad?"

"I'm not."

"You sure?"

"I said, I'm not!"

We both instinctively look in the direction of the reading nook. Neither parent reacts. We continue through the chilly room in silence to the back room, where Jax finally says something. "I thought you were different, that's all. Good to know you're the same as the other kids at school."

"What?"

"She has amyotrophic lateral sclerosis. Not fifty heads or something."

"I wasn't staring like she has fifty heads." I yank at my shirt collar. Was I? I could have been.

"Yes, you were."

My head knows what I'm supposed to do when I hurt someone's feelings—apologize. But my mouth seems to have forgotten and asks, "Does amyotro-a-la. Ummm, Ama-la-la—"

"Just call it ALS," Jax snaps.

I nod. "Does ALS go away?"

"No, it doesn't go away. Don't you know anything?" Jax looks even madder, which doesn't seem fair.

"I know a lot!"

Jax buries his hands in his hair. "If you know so much, why can't you remember me?"

"But I *do* know you."

"No." Jax hiccups. "You don't."

I'm not sure what to say, so I go for the only hiccup cure I know. "Ginger tea helps with the hiccups. I'll get you some."

"I don't want tea." His bottom lip trembles.

"What do you want, then?"

"Nothing."

I pluck a juniper berry from the floor and roll it between my fingers. Berry juice sticks to my fingertips, and I take a deep whiff. It smells of lemon pine cleaner. A memory pops into my mind—lemon, pine, junipers. Somehow, I know it means something. "Are you still mad at me?"

He sucks through his teeth. "I don't know."

"Grams says angry only sticks around until people figure out how to fix things."

Jax exhales with a laugh and wipes his sleeve across his face. "You're so weird."

My lip trembles.

"I didn't mean that in a bad way." He sighs and rubs his thumb against his watch.

"Is that why you slammed the door on me? Because you think I'm weird."

"No." He bends over and picks up a juniper berry. "And I shouldn't have done that." He holds out the berry. "Here, you missed one."

A hollowness aches my bones like a bad case of the flu. We stand awkwardly across from each other, the opposite of two penguins, and I don't like how it feels.

I break the silence. "Do you hate me?"

A rod seems to shoot up his back, and he pulls his hand to his throat. "I could never hate you." His eyelids droop, and his lips twist in a sad half-smile. "I'm really sorry, though. It's like I can't even help anyone anymore. I shouldn't have tried to make you be friends with Billy. It made everything worse."

"Not everything."

"No. Everything." His voice quivers. "You don't remember me anymore. And you and Billy *hate* each other." Jax throws up his hands and lets them drop with a smack on his jeans.

I glance at the juniper berry, and my eyes fly open. Grams' right! Smells are better than pictures for memory. "Why did your mom call you Junior instead of Jax?"

"I don't go by Junior anymore." He stops. "Wait? You

remember me?"

I have memories of us three—Jax, me, and Billy—tossing juniper berries back and forth like they were hot lava, here, in the back room. I know Jax with his big acorn eyes and crooked ear. My ladybug friend who disappeared wasn't a bug. His name wasn't Juniper.

It was Junior.

Holy Monkeys! Does that make Jax one of my Fancies?

No. Jax is real. He was always real, which is worse. Because now I know why Jax wanted to be my friend. So I can unleash my Fancies, and he can share them too. My gut coils like worms crawled in my stomach. But I can't release them. Once they're out again, I may never get them back under control. Then I'm stuck, and Jax will disappear like last time to leave me with the mess. Probably so he can hang out with a friend like Billy.

There's only one thing to do. "I'm sorry. I don't remember you." I drop the juniper berry and squish it with my foot.

Jax crosses his arms. "Yes, you do."

"No. I don't." I twirl a lock of hair around my finger.

"You're lying!" Jax yells. "You're lying right to my face."

The hair gets caught, and I dislodge my finger from the tangle. "N-no. I'm not."

"You are. And you're right about something. You're not my friend. The 'Mere' I knew wasn't a liar." He shoves his hands in his pockets. "You know what? I bet you're the liar Mr. Milke was talking about!"

"Me? I am not!"

"Who cares. You're a liar, and I can't do this anymore. I just . . . I can't."

My toes turn cold. "You can't what?"

"Help you figure out the jinx. Because you don't want to—you're too scared of the truth." Jax yanks his hood down over his eyes. "I don't have time for this. My mom needs me home, not running around trying to help people who are faking it."

15

QUIVERING BLOB OF SLIME

It's been ten days since Jax and I have talked. Even Floss has been acting strange. Yesterday, I asked Floss to go with me to Mr. Dally's. Not in his yard or anything, but to sit with me on the curb across the street. I still have to save Mr. Dally, after all.

Floss just harumphed at me, knocked over juniper berries, and wobbled away.

Mom's also mad. She says she's had enough of my sulking and hanging out on people's curbs, so Grams came up with the idea that we'd all go on a picnic today. Dad's picking me up from school.

"Where's Grams?" I climb in the back.

"She and your mom are putting the last of the picnic basket together. How was school?"

"Fine." I slump down in the backseat, wishing I could ask him how to break a jinx or how to be the kind of friend Jax wants.

We turn the corner to our house, and Dad hollers, "Hold on!" He swerves to the curb and slams on the brakes.

I push up to sit forward and follow his stare. Then I see it—an ambulance—parked in front of our house. Paramedics load Grams into the back; a mask covers her mouth and nose.

Can she breathe?

"Wait here," Dad says and rushes from the car. Mom's talking with the paramedic with a hand over her mouth.

My body turns cold and tingles. This can't be happening.

Dad talks to the driver, and his shoulders drop. He runs around the back and hugs Mom. Before hopping in the back of the ambulance, he points to me in the car, and the doors slam shut behind him. I press my hand to my throat and wait.

The driver flips on spinning lights and the blaring siren. Red strobe lights whirl, setting off a fire alarm of commotion to my brain, twisting my head dizzy.

I stumble from the car and throw up.

My head throbs, and I can't stay any longer. Covering my ears, I run down the street. My feet slap the pavement, my calves start to cramp, but I keep going for what feels like forever. I can't lose Grams. I can't.

Two blocks over. I cut through the gas station and onto the main street, where rows of office buildings line the block. My legs buckle, slamming my knees to the cement. The pain curls me into a sobbing ball on the sidewalk.

Time seems to stand still, and I can't even tell how long I've been laying here. The only sense I have of my physical body is the breeze whipping against my face, sticking to my hot tears.

A deep voice breaks into my bubble. "Mere, is that you?"

Hovering over me is Dr. Richter.

"Grams," I cry out. My back pushes me tighter into a ball.

No matter how hard I try, I can't stretch out.

"Well, you made it to the front of my office." He holds out his hand. "Why don't you come inside?"

I force my body to unfold and push up to standing. Dr. Richter helps me into his office and guides me to the lumpy chair next to a bookshelf full of games.

He hands me a box of tissues. "Meredith, I need to call your parents and let them know you're here. Try to relax. I'll be right back."

I blow my nose.

A few minutes later, he sits in his leather seat and scratches his bushy white beard. "Your parents asked me to let them discuss your Grams with you, okay?"

I nod.

He leans forward over his round belly and asks a question about classes. Or glasses? I try to pay attention, but he stinks of salami. "Your mom says you've had a rough couple of days?"

It's a statement posed as a question. Dr. Richter uses question-statements like this to try and get me to talk. Usually, I don't fall for his trick. But today, my words explode.

"Everything is all messed up. I wanted to help Mr. Dally. And then Jax didn't show up at school. And so I went to his house with Billy, and now they took Grams away in an ambulance!"

Dr. Richter steeples his fingers. "Meredith, I need you to hear me. Nothing you have done has anything to do with what's happening to your Grams."

I can't believe him. Mom says I worry her to death. What if I worried Grams to death?

Outside the window, Mom's car pulls up and parks

at the curb.

"We can discuss more of this at our next session. For now, I think it best you be with your family." Dr. Richter stands, signaling me to get up and go to the door.

I stay seated. "Can I ask a question?"

"Sure."

"Do you only see people who are—?" I spin my finger around my ear, hoping I wouldn't have to say the word.

"I see all kinds of people. Everyone has issues they need to work through."

"Oh." I fidget. "But . . . am I . . . you know?"

"You are fine. You just see things in your own unique way. I'm here to help you figure them out."

"So, I am different."

"Everyone is different." He reaches for the door handle.

This man is supposed to help me! Before the door opens, I blurt, "How can I tell if something is imaginary or real?"

Dr. Richter pulls up his hand and runs it through his beard in that careful way he does when he's trying to come up with a logical explanation about Floss or the other things I see. "Is there something specific you're referring to?"

"What if two kids . . . no, I mean *people*. What if two people walk down the street, and they both see the same thing, like a hummingbird with different wings? Even if no one but those two people can see that hummingbird, does that mean it's imaginary or real?"

"You say both people acknowledge the same bird?"

I nod.

"Then I think it's safe to say that, yes, it is real."

My body collapses as if the bones melted from my body, leaving me a quivering glob of slime on the lumpy chair.

Mom pushes past Dr. Richter and runs to me. She collects me into her arms. "Shhh, it's okay. I've got you."

Dr. Richter holds open the door while Mom carries me to her car. We drive home, where she puts me on the couch in the family room and covers me with a blanket. All I think about is the blanket covering Grams.

"No." I kick it off.

"I'll be right back with your pillow," she says.

I'm so tired. I close my eyes.

16

PLAYING TAG
IN THE SKY

Sunlight shines through the crack between my bedroom curtains. My mouth tastes of dry salt. The last thing I remember is Mom laying me on the couch. *Oh-no.* I sit up.

The blanket I kicked off the couch is folded neatly on my bed. I clutch my pillow to my belly and shuffle down the stairs. Mom and Dad are speaking in hushed tones from the kitchen. When I get in there, Dad rushes over and wraps me in a hug.

"Grams?" I squeak her name.

"She's okay," Dad says. "Just an episode with her heart."

"Because I broke it." I sob.

"No." Dad pulls me from him and looks into my eyes. "Why would you think that?"

I swallow, trying to find air.

"Slow down, Mere." Mom comes up from behind Dad and smooths my hair down. "Grams' heart's not broken. And certainly not from anything you did."

"But it is my fault." I lied to Grams about the fireflies and

129

broke her heart.

The phone rings, and Dad answers. His voice drops. "How many days are we talking about? Okay, Doctor, thank you. My wife and I will be in shortly." He hangs up and looks at Mom and me. "The doctors say she's responding to the medication."

"Can I see her?" I ask.

"Not yet. She's in a special room." Dad moves a stack of napkins on the table, then moves them back to the same spot. The kitchen is cluttered—and not with anything resembling breakfast. Papers and coffee cups are spread across the table. My parents must have been up all night.

Dad grabs a glass from the sink. "Where's your backpack?"

"For what?"

"You're going to be late for the bus."

I look down at my pajamas and blink. "I'm not dressed." Then I realize my mom's wearing her old cotton robe. Did my parents get switched during the night?

"I'm not going to school," I tell him.

"Yes, you are. You have to stay on schedule." Dad pours some orange juice and holds it out for me. "Get ready, and we'll drop you off on our way to the hospital. We'll be with Grams all day and don't want to worry about what you're doing, too."

After I get dressed, I clomp downstairs, and my parents are waiting by the door. Dad's wearing a button-down shirt, one hole off, starting from the second button close to his neck. What's weird is that Mom doesn't even comment on his messy shirt. She yawns and hands him a bag. Is she wearing sweatpants and tennis shoes?

We pile in the car, and Mom peers back at me in the

rearview mirror. "You have your house key?"

I nod.

"Good. Take the bus today. We might not be there when you get home from school, but we'll bring dinner."

After school lets out, I get off at my bus stop, and no one follows me.

I don't want to be home alone, so I cut across the street and head toward the park. I dodge the powerwalking ladies who parade down the footpath, pumping their arms, chins up. They march straight past. I'm invisible again.

I find a spot on the hill and lie flat on the grass. I stare up at the looming clouds. Most cloudy days, Grams and I sprawl out on blankets in our backyard and find shapes. Grams usually makes out the flowers, and I'm good at finding animals or bugs. But today, every cloud looks like mashed potatoes.

I'm about to give up. Then, I notice two clouds floating together. If I tilt my head back and to the left, they almost look like kids—one has a small head, and the other's whole body looks blobby. They move at wind speed, playing tag in the sky.

The breeze shifts and pulls the kids apart, with an expanse of blue sky coming between them. I reach out to pinch them back together, but no luck. When the last wisp of white breaks away, I give up on them and move to stand. My body fights to hold me down, but I press my feet against the ground and push.

I muscle up to a stand, wiping damp grass off my pockets, and hurry off. I shouldn't be here, so I slip back out of the park.

I'm the first one at the house, so I recline on Grams' chair with Jingles curled up beside me on the floor. He sighs every few minutes.

A few hours later, my parents walk through the door.

"We brought food." Dad shakes a greasy fast-food bag. "Chicken nuggets, fries, and extra ketchup packets."

Mom hangs up her coat. "They've moved Grams to another room."

"Can I visit?" My legs tangle in the footrest, trying to get out of Grams' chair. I tumble onto the floor.

"Not tonight." Dad ignores my clumsiness. "It's late. Maybe tomorrow."

I push up to standing. "It's not fair!"

"Don't argue, Meredith." Dad heads to the kitchen.

We sit at the dining room table. Dad hands each of us our meal. Mom nibbles on a chicken nugget without sauce, then looks at the battered lump, like maybe it's not chicken. I dunk a single nugget into my ketchup mound, again and again. I can't eat.

Mom puts her hand on mine. "I'll grab some things. We need to head back to the hospital." She looks at Dad. "Mere needs to see Grams."

I toss my nugget in the box and race to the door. "Can we bring flowers?"

"Not yet," Mom says. "Once we know more, we'll ask what's allowed." She packs a few things while I stand by the front door bouncing on my feet.

We drive miles and park in the visitor's lot before entering through the main hospital. Inside, the air smells damp with pine cleaner and something else. A cat litter box? Pinching my nose to hold back a sneeze, I stay in between my parents through the halls.

Dad gestures to the row of chairs by the nurse's station. "Wait right here, okay?"

I take a seat, keeping my shoes dangling above the dirty floor.

Dad and Mom approach the nurse, and they talk in low voices. The nurse shakes his head and points to the sign.

Visiting hours over.

No! I have to tell Grams I'm sorry.

A lady wearing scrubs swipes her badge on the wall. Double doors open—the barrier separating Grams and me—I slip behind her before they swing close.

The new hall is darker and quieter. I pass two doorways and spot Grams in the third, lying beneath a white sheet, her head raised on a bed. The light behind her hums with electricity through a long bulb. A blue machine connects to her chest with red, white, black, and green wires. Its screen has wiggled lines and numbers on the display.

My vision narrows, and all I see is a worm shape burrowing beneath Grams' skin, protruding from the top of her hand, attaching to a plastic tube, and connecting to a cloudy, fluid-filled bag hanging from the pole next to her bed.

I pull on my shirt collar, trying to suck more air, and yank the necklace chain, too.

The potion!

I rush to her and unclasp the chain. Suddenly, a cold hand touches mine.

"No," she says weakly and shakes her head. "You're all I need."

"Grams!" I crawl into the bed to curl beside her. "Please, don't go away." She pulls me into a snuggle, and I cry so hard my shoulders shake. I'm not sure I will ever stop. And I tell her—I tell her everything, except for my Fancies.

When I finish, she leans back against her pillow. "Well, that's a whole lot of important. But what I want to know is what you learned."

Just then, the nurse rushes into the room, my parents on his heels.

Through gritted teeth, Dad asks, "How'd you get in here?"

Mom crosses her arms. "Mere, this type of behavior has got

to stop. Being worried is no excuse for breaking the rules."

The nurse puts a finger to his lips. "Shh, I think it's time you head home."

I clench Grams' hand. "But we can't leave her."

"I'll be fine," Grams says and pats my hand. "He's probably right. You all get some sleep."

Before I get up, Grams whispers in my ear, "You keep track of that necklace, you hear? Soon, someone's gonna need a special gift like that."

Later that night, I'm tucked into bed when there's a firm knock at my door.

"Come in."

Dad's face pops inside. He smiles, but he looks weary. I don't blame him. He and Mom have been arguing ever since we left the hospital. "Hey, kiddo. You settled in?"

"Mom hates me," I blurt out, sinking into my bed and covering my head with the blanket. The walls of my lavender room seem to shrink in around me. I wrap my arms around my knees, take a deep breath, and exhale. The warm air soothes my throat.

"No. Never." Dad sits on the edge of the bed and rubs my back. "She's concerned."

"But I had to see Grams." My voice sounds muffled. I pull the covers down and say, "It's all my fault. I should've waited for you and Mom in the hospital."

"This isn't about you sneaking into Grams' hospital room.

135

You're not acting like yourself, and it's scaring your mom."

Because I can't be myself.

I nip on my bottom lip, then admit, "I don't have any friends."

Dad hugs me. "I'm sorry, kiddo. Being in fifth grade is hard. But you keep trying. The school year just started. Give it time."

I peek up at Dad, almost too embarrassed to tell him. "Alexa says I'm weird."

"Alexa, hmmm? Well, you tell Alexa we're all a bit weird." He winks. "Don't let a word define you. Besides, I'm proud of my weirdness."

My shoulders stiffen. "You're not weird!"

He chuckles. "So, you know someone else with a flower shop who sells books *and* tea?" He makes a goofy face, and no matter how hard I try, I can't stop a smile.

"Plus, you talk to your flowers," I say.

"I do talk to them. So, lucky for both of us, I'm King Weird."

He's so silly. "But *why* do you talk to them? Are they your friends?"

"Friends?" His eyebrow lifts. "No. But Grams always talked to our plants when I was young, and I do enjoy a good conversation, so maybe they're more like Jingles. Sort of plant-pets."

"Oh." I hoped seeing Fancies was one of those traits we learned about in science, passed down to me, the same as my eye color or hair.

"All I'm trying to say is don't give up on being you."

"Promise, Dad." I hug him tight. "And you don't give up on being you, either."

17

TRUTH IS LIKE CACTUS

Yesterday, we brought Grams home. I'm still scared she's going to have an episode again, but my parents insist that her heart is strong, which makes sense. Grams has the biggest heart of anyone I know.

"Here you go." My hand steady, I pass Grams her favorite sunflower teacup. Jingles snuggles beside her on the mattress, resting his chin on Grams' foot.

Grams takes a sip of tea and creases her forehead. "Did you steep lemon rind in this?" She clinks the cup to the saucer.

"Yes." I take her tea and set it aside. "With green tea. It's good for the heart."

Her eyes close for a moment. "I remember a little boy who used to make tea whenever he had a lot on his mind."

I lay my head on her pillow and tell her about my newest concoction, infused with Roman chamomile flowers from our shop. Since I'm friendless again, all I have is time.

"How are things with Jax?"

I tuck my chin into my chest. "Not good. He's not talking to me."

She clicks her tongue. "Life's hard enough without giving up a good friend."

"I don't know what to do anymore." I curl in closer to her. "Maybe I am afraid, like Jax says." I sniffle. "I want to help Mr. Dally. But I still have to figure out me."

"You can't live your life worrying about tomorrow. You have to do what's right."

"I'm going to help Mr. Dally."

"Good. But you do this on your terms." Grams sits up more in bed and puts her arm around me. "Tell Jax the truth. You never know. He might have truths of his own he needs to share."

"What if telling Jax about me pretending not to remember him makes him not want to help?"

"It's a risk." Grams leans back in bed. "Truth can be like a cactus, full of spines. But at least a cactus is honest about what it is."

"I'm not sure I'm ready."

"Child, who says you're supposed to be ready?" She laughs. "Sometimes life jumps out and hits you on the noggin. Though, sometimes you're not paying the right kind of attention and run smack into a chandelier. Either way, you've got to figure out what to do about the knot on your head."

Grams seems to know the truth of most things, even if she doesn't always make sense. I'm still learning. But I do know I'm done with forgetting friends.

I've been thinking about that a lot. Memories. If you yank a plant by the root, it's like the plant never existed. I figure forgetting is the same as pulling a plant. All those memories I yanked out of me made me a fake—a Meredith who's not real. I want to be real, even if my real is not the regular kind.

Grams nods at me like she knows what I'm thinking, and my heart hiccups. I never want to forget about someone special ever again.

"I have to go." I kiss Grams' cheek and go to my room.

Shutting the door and flicking on the light, I sit at my desk. I know what I have to do. I grab the handful of journal shreds from the top drawer. Then, I cut strip after strip of plastic tape and put the list back together again.

When I finish the task, I go over the plan. I've spent the last few years of my life pretending I don't see things. But being ordinary isn't for me. Things are going to change. It's time I learn more about the jinx. It's time to stop being afraid, and there's only one place I know to get answers.

I put on pajamas and climb into bed, focusing on old friends. Here goes everything.

"Please. Sorry. Thanks," I say.

Tiny pastel bunnies hop overhead, *sunflower yellow, piglet pink, lime green* . . . I repeat the colors the same way I used to until my eyelids flutter closed.

My eyes open, and I'm inside a tunnel. I swirl in a kaleidoscope of colors; each rotation makes me dizzier and dizzier as I fall deeper within. When I was younger, I visited this place all the time, so I know if I'm going to land on my feet,

I need to flap my hands and slow myself before I hit the bottom.

When I land, I fall to my knees in a field of flowers.

Crushed petals stick to my pajamas like a mess of sewn patches. I brush them off and follow the same crooked path I've taken so many times before.

My legs move in slow motion. I'm walking through a thick fog, leaving a trail of yellows, oranges, and blues behind me. By now, my thighs should have the strength to take on this slope, but my legs are still stick thin. Each step I take up the grassy hill is a struggle. I extend my legs to gain distance. On the other side of this hill is an amusement park.

At the top of the hill, I catch a glimpse of the brightly colored Ferris wheel, each seat filled with animals of all sorts enjoying a beautiful day. A pair of porcupines, wearing straw hats, wave. Good 'ole Cliff and Irene always have a friendly greeting for me. I wave back and make my way down the hill.

As I step through the vine-covered gates, time zooms forward, then back to regular speed. The scent of roasted peanuts cooked on a smoldering fire waft into my nostrils and fill my head with good memories.

I step up to the Ferris wheel platform and wait for my turn. The gold coin I always find in my pajama pockets is enough to pay the tortoise for the ride.

"Welcome back, Miss Dandy." Mr. Tortoise takes my coin and pulls the lever to slow the giant wheel.

"Thank you." I sit next to a hyena who can't stop laughing. I giggle with her, and we ascend higher and higher. The whole park is visible from the top. Ms. Hyena nudges me and hands me her binoculars. Through the lenses, I spot a pair of shimmering

wings belonging to a long beak with a top hat.

Mr. Milke! He's tossing a baseball at a painted clown's mouth, trying to knock out its wooden teeth. This dream is where I first met him. That was before he and my other Fancies started showing up everywhere.

As the Ferris wheel rolls to the bottom, I yell out to Mr. Tortoise, "Hey, can you let me off?" He nods, but the wheel goes around once more before stopping. When it does, I hand back the binoculars to Ms. Hyena and clamber from the seat, racing to the clown carnival game.

Mr. Milke tosses me a ball with his white-gloved hand. "One shot, Dandy. You're the best at this game. Now, concentrate. There are two teeth left to knock out."

I can't throw worth beans, and the ball is too small for my hands, but I can tell he's counting on me to get those last teeth so he can win a prize. I wind up the ball and throw. It spins in slow motion, responding to the amusement park's time warp, dipping and diving, about to fall off course when *Bam!* I jump up and down as the last teeth fall. Sharp whistles blow, and bells cling and clang.

Mr. Milke claps his hands and points to a stuffed giraffe.

How odd. The last time I was here, the prizes seemed larger.

Patiently, I wait for the carnival rabbit to remove the prize from the hanger and hand it to Mr. Milke. The giraffe is almost twice Mr. Milke's size. I'm surprised he can carry it.

"Can I talk to you?" I ask.

"I assumed it's why you came to see me."

My stomach knots. "I'm sorry I gave up knowing you."

"You've had a lot on your mind. Shall we have a seat?"

Mr. Milke points to a row of picnic tables on the park midway. "Over there."

He buzzes alongside me and tips his top hat to everyone we pass.

Annabelle, the daffodil from the nursery, works the candy shop, dipping red apples into caramel and topping them with milk chocolate. She sprinkles a few raisins on before the chocolate hardens. Last time I visited here, Annabelle worked at the cotton candy shop.

Mr. Milke inhales, filling his chest and puffing out his wings. The tuxedo feathers ruffle, and his head bobs. He winks at Annabelle. She giggles and waves to us both.

Once we pass by the candy shop, he exhales with a cough. His face flushes from holding his breath in so long. I take his giraffe, pinching the stuffed animal prize between my fingernails, and set it on the table before taking a seat.

"What can I do for you, Dandy?"

"Why do you call me Dandy?" I blurt out since it's what confuses me most, other than why I can see him when I'm awake and how Jax fits into all of this.

"It's short for Dandy-lion."

"I figured since the shop is mine. But why?"

"You don't like dandelions?" He bobs his head sideways and stares at me curiously.

"I do. I just don't understand."

He sighs. "I have never figured out why humans must understand everything."

My shoulders droop. "Then, I am human."

"Of course. Why wouldn't you be?"

Tears sting my eyes, and I squeeze them back. Nothing about me is extraordinary—I'm just not.

"But you are," he answers my thoughts, and this time it doesn't freak me out. "You have a gift. One I worried you had lost. I admit to being concerned at first, but I'm glad Jax chose to remind you."

"A gift? What kind?"

"How do I explain?" He taps his gloved hand against his needle-like beak. "Ah! I know. Have you ever met a child who plays with imaginary friends?"

"Yes." Is he making fun of me?

"Right. Well, humans—all humans—are born with the ability to perceive our world. As young children, their minds are filled with innocence and fun. No one thinks twice when children talk to us. We're their make-believe friends." He zooms straight into the air and loops twice, the tips of his wings vibrating and chirping, then he lands back on the bench with a bow.

I suppose I should clap for him, but now I'm super worried. Mr. Milke thinks he's make-believe.

He shakes out his wings and continues like it doesn't matter if he is or not. "But as children grow, their ability to see our world changes, mostly because it's no longer acceptable for them to notice us. Though sometimes they no longer choose to." He swipes a tear with his wingtip and smiles bravely.

"Why can I see you now? I'm almost eleven."

"Yes, you are. How quickly you all grow. Occasionally, rare humans are born. Humans have all sorts of names for these children."

I thought of all the names I've been called and cringe.

"They are the ones who can see us well into their adulthood. We call them our 'Dreamers.' You are part of our world."

"Me?" I point to myself.

He bobs his head.

"Oh." My voice squeaks. "Can I do magic? Like, do I get a wand?"

Mr. Milke chuckles. "No, Miss Dandy. That's a magician."

I frown. "I'd really like a wand."

"Me too!" He waves his hand in the air as if casting a spell, then drops his arm. "But a wand cannot see. Your particular sensitivities appear to allow you to see the tiniest details in things, like our world."

I can't imagine why anyone would want to see details that make them friendless. I shuffle from one foot to another, thinking of how my life would have been if I'd never met Floss. "So, are all sensitive kids Dreamers?"

"No. Not all of them. But those other sensitive children might be other fine things." He pulls out a piece of butterscotch candy the size of an ice cream sprinkle from his sash pocket and holds it out to me. I shake my head, and he pops the treat into his mouth.

"How am I part of your world if I didn't remember it the last time I saw you?"

"Perhaps you needed time to figure out if we were still part of *your* world.

I bite my cheek. "Jax isn't sensitive, I don't think, so how does he see you?" I ask. "And why can't he see you when I'm not with him?"

"Jax can see us because he believes in you. So long as you

choose to see, so will he."

Jax believes in me? He *is* my friend! My stomach drops. And I'm a lousy friend. All Mr. Milke did was remind me of that. "So, this is all real?"

He winks. "As real as I am." Distracted by something, he tilts an ear upward and listens. "I would love to discuss this further, but we don't have time. Mr. Dally needs your help."

Mr. Dally's house pops into my mind. "I know. Jax and I are the only ones who can help him. Do you know how we break the jinx? I'm finally ready to ask Billy for help."

Mr. Milke's lips move, and my shoulders shake. A loud beep drowns out his response. *My alarm?* I feel soft hands, like Mom's, and the gentle shake grows stronger. I can barely see Mr. Milke. My vision tries to adjust. I try to push the hands away, but the grip tightens.

Without warning, I'm thrust back through the colorful tunnel, spinning round and round, even though I want to stay.

18

PUDDLE OF RAINBOW OIL

When I show up downstairs in the morning, my family is gathered around the table for our special Saturday breakfast.

"Morning." I sit beside Grams and grab a pancake, slathering on smooth peanut butter until it melts.

Dad says, "You ready for work?"

"Do I have to?"

Everyone stops and stares at me. Usually, I'm excited about working with him. But I need to talk to Billy. "I mean, I want to. But I need to run to Billy's house. Can I come by right after?"

Mom puts a few strawberries on my plate. "It's nice the two of you are getting along."

Dad's eyes narrow, and he takes a bite of his eggs. Chewing with his mouth open, he says, "Be there by ten."

Outside, the fall air is crisp, and I bundle up with my sweater.

Gold and red autumn leaves cover the neighborhood. The trees stand stark, almost bare. The transition used to make me sad, watching plants wither and dry. But Dad says that fall isn't the end. It's the beginning of change. Plants going dormant is nature's way of allowing the earth to grow back stronger.

Change isn't always bad.

I hop over the cracks and race to Billy's house. The front window blinds in his living room are wide open. I sneak across the lawn to the patio and bob my head up to peek inside. Billy's slumped on the couch in front of the television.

Mr. Simpson storms into the room and turns it off. The vein in his forehead bulges like an earthworm crawled under his flushed skin. Maybe it is an earthworm? He doesn't act happy as he knocks Billy's feet off the coffee table and stands over him. Mr. Simpson's lips move, and he jabs his thumb to the back of the house.

A sadness bunches around Billy's eyes, then he gets to his feet and shuffles from the room. I've seen Billy with that same look before, the day his mom left for good—after he finally stopped crying.

A few minutes later, the garage door opens. The car door slams, and his dad's cherry-red racecar backs out from the garage.

I throw myself down flat on the porch with my fingers up. I figure since posing your arms makes you resemble a tree, then maybe posing your fingers looks like grass, which I know is silly. There isn't any grass on the porch. Pretty sure this is never going to work.

Mr. Simpson is alone in the car and doesn't notice me. His

engine revs and tires squeal; he peels out the long driveway. The garage door closes behind him, and I jump to my feet. Creeping up to the rose bushes, I roll a dried stem between my fingertips. It feels sad and lonely, like it hasn't eaten properly for a long time—*poor flower.*

Careful, I unclasp my necklace and open the bluebell drawstring. Inside, the potion swirls like a puddle of rainbow oil caught in a spin drain. It hardens into chalk clumps and smells sweet. I hold the bluebell sack over a bush but worry freezes my hand. What if using the potion sets off a Fancies swarm?

The chalky powder's honey scent wafts into my nose. I know it's ready. Yet, my fingers turn numb. It's harder than I thought to ignore this fear. But I can't keep being afraid.

I shake free from my fright and sprinkle the potion onto the dead flower. I thought I only had enough to dust one rose, but it keeps trickling out of the bag, so I work my way down the flower beds along the front row. Amazing! One teeny flower bag covered the entire thing.

"There." I shake out the last bit as if it's the most normal thing I've ever done. And I wait.

If this potion is magical, then the flowers should grow. That will make Billy agree to unjinx Mr. Dally. Simple. Just in case, I cross both fingers and toes and wait for something to happen.

The mangled stems stay dry and dead.

Huh? Might take a while. I check my watch—shoot—I'm almost out of time if I'm gonna make it to Dad's shop. It's now or never—deep breath. I creep to Billy's white front door and raise my hand to grasp the knocker—a lion's head with sharp teeth holds a brass ring.

As I move closer, Predator Cat gapes his mouth. *Holy Monkeys!* Not again.

"You stop that," I tell the lion, and it yawns before shutting its eyes.

"Nice kitty." I pat its head and rap three times.

Billy opens the door, his eyes puffy and bloodshot. "What do you want?"

"I need your help."

"Not a chance, freak." Billy starts to close the door.

"Wait!" I shove my foot in the opening to stop him, crushing my toes a little. "So what if I am a freak? Everyone's different. And you're not bad. Well, you are, but you don't have to be. Come with me."

"I'm not going with you anywhere. You're a big mouth."

"Me?" My jaw drops like it's loaded down with a mouthful of pennies. Is he serious? "You're the one who told the whole second grade about my Fanc—I mean, imaginary friends."

"Because you told everyone my mom left my dad." Billy wipes his sleeve across his nose.

"No, I-I—" Wait, did I? Cold splashes me like I did a polar bear plunge. Goosebumps spring on my arms, and I can't hold back a shiver.

A memory creeps into my mind, whizzing by in snapshots.

Click—his house.

Click—his mom crying on the couch.

Click—*me*—telling the teacher in front of the class.

Click—the kids laughed.

Oh, no! Billy cried.

A hollow ache radiates from my stomach. "I'm-I'm sorry."

Billy's lower lip quivers. "Why did you tell?"

"I was in second grade. I didn't know I wasn't supposed to."

But I do now.

Maybe I can take it back?

Without a blink, I stare Billy in the eyes, so he knows I mean it. "I shouldn't have told anyone what happened at your house. I was wrong, and I'm sorry. Sometimes I blurt things out, and I don't mean to. Can you stop the jinx now?"

Billy's head jerks back. His face freezes.

"Mr. Dally? Dead Man's Castle?"

He shrugs. "There's no way to stop it. I tried."

"Are you sure?"

"Yes."

This is not promising. I try a different approach. "But why would you want to jinx Mr. Dally in the first place?"

"I didn't mean to." He shuffles his feet. "I was, I don't know. Mad. The Dallys had the best garden, you know, the way my mom's was before . . ." He wraps his arms to hug himself.

I pull my foot out of the doorframe. "Maybe if you tell me how you did it, we can figure out how to stop the jinx."

"I just." He shivers. "I was walking by, and they had this huge sunflower. So, I stopped to look at it because I like sunflowers. Then, I saw their roses, and I got mad. I can't remember what I said, but I think I called them ugly, and I wished bugs would eat holes in them until they shriveled up and died." Billy chews on his knuckle. "But then Mrs. Dally died. And I couldn't take it back. I swear, I didn't mean to hurt anyone."

Whenever Billy gets caught lying about picking on me, his ears redden, and he argues loud. I lean close to him and check both his ears.

He steps back. "What are you doing?"

"Nothing." His ears aren't red. He's telling the truth. "Would you help if I told you I might have found a jinx reverse?" I pluck a dry twig from the rose bush. "It was on this website called *Floggy's Cures for a Jinx.*"

"Floggy's what?"

"Cures for a Jinx. All you have to do is walk backward in front of the house and do the jinx blocker in reverse. Then the jinx should break."

Billy shivers. "No. I'm not messing with that stuff anymore. You figure it out." He turns back inside.

"If you help me, I'll replant your flowers out front."

He stops.

"And I'll come by to give them the right nutrients and water." When Billy shakes his head, I add, "For two months."

He rubs the back of his neck. "Why should I believe you?"

My chest puffs. "Because I keep my promises."

Billy snorts. "You remember when you would make us do that hummingbird-wing-flutter-swear-thing to keep a promise?" A smirk creeps on his lips. "That was lame."

"I . . . uh." My neck snaps to Billy. "Wait! I thought you said you never heard of Mr. Milke?"

His nose scrunches. "Who's this Mr. Milke you keep asking about?"

"Never mind."

Billy doesn't remember him. He remembers Jax and me. I'm the one who forgot we were friends. What kind of terrible friend am I? I got too busy trying to make myself regular, and I almost lost everything.

"Fine," Billy says, "I'll help. But only if you bring the rosebushes back to life, too."

Roses were his mom's favorite flower.

"And this jinx business has to wait until Tuesday. I'm grounded. For going to Jax's." Billy glares at me like he wants to remind me he's in trouble because he helped me.

"Deal." I stick out my hand to shake. He watches me for what feels like forever before he takes my hand. I ignore the sweaty slick.

"Deal." He shakes once, squeezing tight, then yanks his hand back.

Behind him, green vines snake up the house and spiral to the rooftop. I pretend not to notice when sunny yellow flowers burst open and smile.

19

LEMON DROP HORSES

Sundays aren't always fun days, especially when my mind's on things other than working at Dad's shop.

"Dad, do you need me to water the plants?" I sweep the last heap of dirt into the dustpan.

"Certainly," he says, rearranging the books on the store shelf. "Don't forget to talk to the blooms."

"I won't." I fill the can to the top and carry it to the back room. Water sloshes on the floor. I hum to myself and sprinkle the front row of flowers. With my last chore complete, I set the can on the floor and check to make sure the note is in my pocket. Here goes nothing. "You can come out now." I spread my arms wide and spin in a circle.

Glitter and sparkles swirl around me and sweep into a rainbow of colors. I spin faster and faster, mixing violet, sunflower, and periwinkle together until I'm dizzy.

Pop-crack-spark.

An old-fashioned merry-go-round sprouts from the center

of the room; the walls are replaced by an outdoor amusement park. Aboard the carousel, cinnamon hard candy ponies and lemon drop horses glisten in the sunlight. Pipe organ music fills my ears, and the sweet smell of freshly spun cotton candy drifts into my nostrils. I take a deep sniff and sigh. Why would I ever want to forget this place?

Mr. Milke flutters by my face. "Good afternoon, Miss Dandy." He lands on top of one of the giant lollypops planted in the grass and tips his top hat.

"Good afternoon." I curtsy.

Annabelle the daffodil blows me a kiss and giggles from her red-and-white striped candy stand.

"Things are going well, I assume?" Mr. Milke's high-pitched voice is soothing.

"Not yet. But I have a plan. Can I give Annabelle a note?"

"Certainly."

I bring her the paper folded in my pocket and whisper in her ear. When I return, Mr. Milke beams at me. But he shouldn't be proud yet—I'm not sure my plan will work. The first step is to get Jax back tomorrow.

"But you will," he says, again reading my mind.

"I hope so. There's this website from someone named Floggy? And it says only the Jinx Master can break a jinx, which is Billy, and he's agreed to help." Plucking a grass blade, I stick it in my mouth. *Holy monkeys, that's gross!* I spit it out. Why does Jax chew grass?

"Floggy?" Mr. Milke shoves his hands in his sash pocket and rocks back and forth. "Now, why does the name sound—" His head pivots, and he hollers, "Floss?"

156

Floss peeks from under a bag of popcorn, munching on a kernel. He blinks and points to himself.

"Can you come out here, please?"

Floss skittishly steps toward us and then dodges back under the bag. *Kssch!*

Mr. Milke chuckles and kneels. "You're not in trouble. I need a little information. Can you help?"

Floss shuffles out from under the bag. Standing in front of us, he crosses his six feet back and forth with a sheepish grin. I keep my stare trained on him.

Mr. Milke clears his throat. "Is there something you would like to tell us?"

Floss shakes his head *no,* which wiggles his backend like a wet puppy shake.

"Are you certain?"

Floss droops his head. *Kscchhh.*

"I see." Mr. Milke scratches his featherhead. "Anything else?"

Floss spins in circles, his legs crisscrossing so fast he can barely keep his feet untangled. Watching him makes me dizzy until Floss trips into a somersault and lands belly up on the floor. *Fleeep!* He farts.

My cheeks burn. Floss did that on purpose!

Except his cheeks are pink, and he's acting bashful, so maybe not.

Floss points to the ceiling. *Ksch-kzzing.*

Smart move. Distraction. Why didn't I think of that? I don't want to embarrass Floss, so I pretend I didn't hear him pass gas and follow to where he's pointing. Though, I can't understand his hissing.

Mr. Milke does. "And I am certain she would thank you. But do you think perhaps you can allow her to work it out on her own?"

Floss lowers his bug eyes. For a moment, I feel sorry for him, but I'm betting he's up to something.

Frweenddd, Floss finally says.

"Work what out on my own?" I ask Mr. Milke.

Mr. Milke flutters his wings. "Nothing important. Floss and I are having a little disagreement."

It doesn't look like any disagreement I've ever heard.

Floss winks at me and scuttles beneath the popcorn stand.

"Well, this settles that." Mr. Milke brushes his gloves together. "It appears Floss also believes you are capable of working it out on your own."

"Why? What did he say?"

"I believe he said, 'friend.'"

"Huh?"

"He takes a bit to understand. The w's mean—" He brushes his hand away. "Well, it isn't important."

"It is, though." I cross my arms. "I get in a lot of trouble because of him."

Mr. Milke chuckles. "Floss means well, especially when it comes to you. Take heart, Miss Dandy. He pranks you because it's what he knows best. Had he behaved, perhaps we would not be having this conversation now."

"Floss stole—" I'm about to explain how Floss stole my grape juice, when a giraffe leans its long neck down and plops a bag of peanuts into my open hand. Its dark purplish tongue slurps back in its mouth. Drool oozes down the bag's folds as the giraffe meanders away.

"Thank you," I holler, placing the bag on the floor and wiping my hands on my jeans. "Can I ask you a question?"

"You always do." Mr. Milke wiggles his handlebar mustache.

"We all used to come here, right? Jax, me, and Billy?" I remember now the three of us had playdates together. That's what Jax meant by Billy being 'one of us.' "So why can't Billy see you anymore?"

"Ah. A difficult question." He rubs his chin. "But the answer remains simple. One must believe things are possible, to do the impossible. I suspect Billy does not believe he can even manage the possible yet."

"Uh, okay." What does that mean? "Can you come with me tomorrow? I could use your help to get Jax back."

"I believe you will." He preens his wings.

Another non-answer.

I consider asking again, but that uses up another question. Asking two at a time is okay, but three is rude, and I have another important one. Arms wide, I gesture to the amusement park. "Is all this a dream, and that's why you call us 'Dreamers?'" Combining two questions into one makes it only a one and a half, which isn't too rude.

"Ah, wonderful question." He taps his forehead. "We call you our Dreamers because most keep us tucked away in their dreams. It feels safer to visit us that way. Rarely does a Dreamer have your ability to project us into their world. Even then, you should only see us when you want to."

Then I'm unique? Unless "rarely" means millions. Are there any statistics on Dreamers? The word "rarely" also means seldom occurring, so I'm going with unique.

Kssch Haw! Floss is riding the carousel, flailing on top of a polka-dotted saddle while pretending he's on a bucking bronco. Joining him looks tempting, and the horse doesn't seem to mind. No. I don't have time for fun today.

"But if I'm only supposed to see you when I want, how come Floss shows up whenever?"

"Meredith!" Dad's voice hollers from a distance. "Where are you?"

"Oh, I gotta go!" I scramble toward the exit sign. "See you later, everyone."

All of the animals stop what they're doing and wave. "Bye, Dandy. Bye."

Yellow lights blink, and I follow the arrows past the gate and up the hill. Floss scuttles after me. A rainbow of colors surrounds me, trapping me in a vortex. My limbs move slow, fast, slow. I reach the top of the hill and climb into a white billowing cloud.

My lashes flutter, and I'm back in Dad's shop. Yawning, I stretch and stagger from the comfy spot on a pile of burlap seed bags. "Coming," I yell to my dad.

20

MY FRIEND, ANNABELLE

Today's Monday!

Nervous, I wiggle from the toasty sheets and jump from bed, racing to the bathroom to brush my teeth. I feel a glimmer of optimism. Because no matter how my apology goes, I'm going to come clean to Jax and explain why I lied about my Fancies.

I rummage through the hamper and pull out a shirt with a dancing raccoon. It's got a little stain, but that's okay, I'll wear it anyway. Brush in hand, I sit on the bathroom counter and take time fixing my hair. *Holy Monkeys.* My hair tangles the same as yesterday. Grabbing the tube of hair goo, I head to my parents' room.

Mom's sitting on her bathroom counter, staring into the mirror and swiping a wand of mascara over her lashes. Will I ever be as beautiful as her?

"Meredith, you're going to be late."

"I won't."

She pulls the wand away from her lashes. "Do you need

161

something?"

"Can you do my hair?"

Mom blinks at me and puts away the mascara. "You want *me* to do your hair?" When I nod, her rose-red lips break into a smile. "Here." She pulls out her makeup chair, and I sit. She glides the brush through the tangles and smooths down my locks.

"One more thing. Do you mind?" she asks with the tiniest grin. When I nod, she pulls out a black bag with a yellow bow from under the cabinet and hands it to me. "I know how much you love these."

My heart leaps. Inside is bubblegum lip balm.

"May I?" she asks, and when I lift my chin, she smooths on the pink tint for me. "There." Mom whirls me back around to face the mirror.

My face drops. "You didn't do anything different to my hair."

"Why would I? Your hair's perfect. Just needed a little smoothing."

I finger comb through the soft strands and realize I do like cotton ball hair.

"Thank you." I leap from the seat and hug her tight.

"You're very welcome," Mom says, hugging me back.

I could hug her forever, but I have to go. "Can you drive me to school today? I have something I need to do early." When she says yes, I grab the flowers I prepared last night from my room and head to the car.

My feet tap the bottom of the floor mats all the way to school.

"Have a nice day," Mom says, and I scoot from the car, careful not to drop the bud vase. Class doesn't start for thirty minutes—enough time if I work quickly.

I climb the steps to my school and enter the quiet hallway. The next hall over, I give the nod.

Kssch! Floss shimmies out of my jacket pocket and darts down the hall. I follow until we find Jax's classroom and his desk.

"Good job," I tell Floss for sniffing out Jax's desk and situate the vase of forget-me-nots to fit careful inside. Floss disappears, and I head straight to the computer lab to research the *Farmers' Almanac* before school starts. Everything's either falling into place, or soon will.

When school finally lets out, I dash to the bus line and find Mr. Jennings. "Can you please give this to Jax? My dad is driving me home today."

"Sure," he says, taking the card from me and the single perfect blue flower with a yellow middle. "I'll make sure he gets it."

"Thank you."

Dad is waiting in his car at the curb, and I hop inside.

"Your mom says you're going to the park with Jax after school?"

"Yes." I lock and unlock my ankles.

He lets me off at Jax's bus stop and leans out the window. "And what time did you promise to be home by?"

"Before the streetlights come on." I hold out my pinkie, and he locks his with mine.

"Don't forget. Have fun."

When his car turns the corner, I rush back to the bus stop and kneel on the sidewalk to peer at a crack. "Where are you?" I whisper.

A tiny giggle comes from the sidewalk behind me, and I spin around. Annabelle blinks her green lashes at me from the next crack over.

"Thank you for coming," I tell her.

She puckers her yellow trumpet petals and blows me a kiss. "Are you ready?"

She giggles.

"The first one goes right here." I point.

Annabelle bends her stem at the shoulder and touches the crack—a dandelion sprouts. I place a folded card with a drawn arrow beside the stem and move a few sidewalk cracks down. "And here."

Annabelle wilts into the sidewalk crack and pops up new and fresh in the next spot, dipping her stem shoulder to the ground—another dandelion sprouts. I add another arrow. We plant dandelions down the block and across the street, creating a path into the park and over the grassy hill, ending at the swing set where we add the final touch.

"Here."

Annabelle tucks her petals tight, then flings them wide. Beside the swings grows a juniper bush.

I lean down. "You're a good friend, Annabelle."

With a pleased giggle, she disappears.

Alone once again, my stomach moths churn and flitter to my chest. To keep calm, I sit on a swing, pumping my legs, pushing myself toward the sky. And I wait.

Then I swing, and I swing for what seems like *forever*.

Check my watch—ten past five o'clock. Time's about up. The streetlights come on at six. Now, I know for certain what I didn't want to believe. Jax doesn't see the dandelions. He can't find me because he doesn't believe in me anymore.

I lost Jax.

My arms wrap around the chains, and my head hangs low. Inside my sneakers, my toes push and pull against the ground; small sways are all I can muster. Back and forth, going nowhere. I think back to the first day of school. Back then, the worst thing that could happen was that I wouldn't make friends. Now, I know better. Being friendless is easier.

I didn't realize how bad losing a best friend can hurt.

21

OH, FLOSS

I can't wait anymore—time to head home.

Chills shiver through me, and I pry my fingers from the chain.

The swing beside me squeaks. I jerk my head up, and my heart soars. "I didn't think you would come."

Jax stares ahead, swaying on the swing. "I didn't think so either."

I twist back and forth in my seat, watching leaves rustle and tumble across the ground. "I wasn't telling the truth at my dad's shop."

"Ya, I know."

"I'm sorry."

"Well, I had my reasons, and they weren't so honest, either." Jax frowns. "Let me show you something." He pulls a folded picture from his jacket pocket and holds the photo out for me to see. It's faded yellow with a fold line down the middle.

I grit my teeth to keep from snatching the wrinkled photo

from Jax's hand. I'm itching to smooth the creases out. The picture is of a smiling family at the beach. The boy in the middle is about five or six with a buzz haircut and big acorn cap eyes. I recognize Mrs. Cooper, not in a wheelchair, and she's holding hands with a man who looks like an older version of Jax.

"He's my dad," Jax says and taps his watch. "This was his too. He got in an accident, which is the last time I saw you before this year." He tucks the photo back in his jacket and fidgets with his thumbs. "We moved away after . . ." He shrugs.

"That's so sad." My heart searches for something better to say, but there are no words, magical or not, to stop the pain of loss.

Be brave.

I slide off the swing and pluck a juniper berry. Crushing it between my fingers releases a lemony-pine scent with a hint of fresh-cut grass. Memories. I pick a juniper berry and hand it to Jax. "I *do* know you. You're Juniper."

He grins.

That's how I figured everything out. The berries Floss spilled everywhere in my dad's shop. That pesky beetle made a mess to remind me.

I sit back on the swing and twist to face him. "We were friends. I—well, the truth was I thought you were a ladybug. I don't know why. And I think I used to call you Juniper, right?"

He nods.

"Then, when you went away, I missed you. I must have missed you so much it hurt less to forget you. I know you were trying to help Mr. Dally and Billy. Even me. But I didn't want to be stuck with Fancies and not a real friend. So, I lied." My

voice trembles.

"We can find another way to help Mr. Dally."

"That's the thing," I tell him. "Fancies aren't the real problem. It was me, trying to hide them, even from myself. To be someone that I'm not."

"You're fine—"

I hold up my hand. "So, here's the thing. It's up to me to choose when and where I see my Fancies, always has been. Them coming back? That's not on you. I understand now why you wanted to be Billy's friend. You can even be his friend and not mine if you want. But I need to help Mr. Dally. And I promise if you'll give me another chance, cross my heart, I'll never forget you again." My finger draws an X over my heart.

And suddenly, every moment I spent without Jax comes tumbling back into my head. As if the clouds release a watering can of tears down my cheeks.

How could I have forgotten him? *My Juniper.*

Moment after moment, they fall. I can't stop them. A breeze cools the hot trickles and sticks the salt to my raw skin. It seems like forever before the chill finally slows my tears, and I catch my breath. I pull a tissue from my pocket to dab my eyes. "I'm sorry."

"It's all right." He sniffles.

I peek at him. His eyes are damp. I tuck the tissue in my pocket. "Why don't you like being called Junior?"

He sighs. "Because I'm not technically a junior anymore, I'm the only one mom has left."

I press my hand to my heart. How could I have been so blind to other people's problems? I need to be a better friend, starting right now. "She can have me too. And my family. Okay?"

Jax holds out his fist, and I close mine, bumping his knuckles the way friends do. It feels better than I ever imagined, and I don't want to waste one more minute being mopey with Jax.

In a flash, I hop back up and pluck another juniper berry, tossing it in the air and slicing it in half with an imaginary sword. "On guard." I point the sword to him.

Jax's face gleams, then his lip curls into a sneaky grin. He leaps from his swing, grabs a handful of berries, and tosses them—*Snap*—his sword appears. He twists and lunges like a trained knight, slicing each one before they fall to the ground.

"Let's go!" I race to the top of a hill and hold the sword up.

Jax takes long strides until he's right beside me.

I drop the sword to my side and ask him, "But why would I call you Juniper? It doesn't make sense."

"Because you couldn't pronounce Junior."

"But I don't understand. Why didn't you tell me we were friends that first day at the lunch table?"

"I tried to." Jax leans against his sword on the grass. "But each time, you wouldn't let me, and I knew something wasn't right. You didn't recognize me, and you didn't believe in anything fun anymore. That started to make me wonder if I made everything up."

"Sure. I get it." Before I can decide if I should ask, I blurt out, "Have you been to Mr. Milke's amusement park lately?"

"No. Until the other day, I stopped seeing anything fun since the day my dad—" He swallows. "I guess I convinced myself I made up the Dandy-lion shop."

"How can we both make up the same place?"

"We can't. But I couldn't see it without you. The shop disappeared." He hops onto a dirt mound and balances, holding his sword out to me. "You're the key. Probably because you were the one who always came up with the cool adventures. Remember when we rode on cleaning buckets and defeated the snow pirates?"

I cross my sword to Jax's with a *clink*. "Of course!" Now, I do.

Jax grins. "Which is why I brought you to the Dandy-lion—I needed to make sure. The thing is, only you can change it to your store."

"Sometimes, I can't. Some days it's just Dad's shop."

"Maybe that's because Mr. M.'s busy with other kids, and they need to shut the place down?"

Mr. Milke did say there were other Dreamers.

"Don't worry." Jax stows his sword into the sheath on his belt. "I'm sure it'll be there when you need it."

I sheath my sword, as well. "Billy used to hang out with us."

"He did. What happened to him? He used to be so much fun, and now he's angry."

"Billy probably would have told you himself. But so you know, I used Mr. Milke's potion on his flowers."

"You did? Really?"

"Yes." A thought nudges me. I can't focus on what it is. *Ohhh.* I cringe. "I'm sorry for staring at your mom the other day. It wasn't because of her wheelchair. She has a pretty smile. I worried Floss might steal her teeth."

"Floss?" His eyes widen, and he laughs. "I almost forgot him. Is the little guy still giving you a hard time?"

"The worst." I wiggle my shoulders to get rid of the heebie-jeebies. A feeling of relief follows, making them lighter. Finally, someone gets me. "He stole another one of my teeth. It was a baby tooth, but still."

The truth about Floss is he started showing up when I lost my first baby tooth. I remember because I spent all day worrying about the tooth fairy breaking into my room and couldn't sleep. And *pop*, in a sweet cloud of funnel cake, Floss appeared. He snuck under the pillow, tied the tooth to a string of my favorite cinnamon dental floss, and hauled it away—which is why I named him Floss.

"What do you need a baby tooth for anyway?" Jax elbow-nudges me.

"Nothing. But it's mine."

"True." He gives me a grin, and I swear his eyes sparkle. "And this here is what I missed most about you, what I meant by a *good* weird. You being you. Not what you think everyone wants you to be."

"Kids don't want me to be me." I frown.

"Who cares. I like you better this way."

"I do too."

Jax rubs his neck and looks off for a moment. "We don't have to be friends with Billy like we were before. He's changed. I just, well . . ."

"No, you're right. We need to give him a chance," I tell him. "Besides, we still need Billy. He's agreed to help Mr. Dally."

I figured something else out—when Jax's mom lost her husband, she must have been sad like Mr. Dally—that's why Jax wanted to help Mr. Dally in the first place.

"So, this is happening?" Jax asks. "We're back on?"

"Yep. Tomorrow, we're going to free Mr. Dally."

Jax walks me home, and I think about everything on the way and realize I've always had friends. Maybe not regular friends, like other kids, but they were there. It was me who changed when I stopped being a good friend. Grams was right. This time I hit my own head. And it's not only Mr. Dally I need to make things up to; there are other friends too. That list starts now.

22

Boo!

It's "Taco Tuesday" in the cafeteria, which means long lines and guacamole. Avocados don't have a gross smell—or any smell—so I am not distracted. I can't imagine why anyone would eat them mashed, though. Guacamole looks like green peas in baby jars.

I slip two quarters into the vending machine, grab my grape juice, and cut through the crowded cafeteria.

"I like your shirt," Molly says from a table full of girls.

"Thank you." I notice her sweater has a bunny on the front. "I like yours, too."

Isabel scoots over and pats the bench like she's making room between her and Alexa. I offer a little smile but pass by, not sure how else to react.

From our regular table, Jax waves me over. He's sitting next to Billy.

I take my usual spot and lean across the table to them. "Today's the day. Meet me in front of the Dally's after school."

Billy drops his taco onto the table.

"You in, or you out?" I try to ignore the clumpy green yuck stuck on the side of his mouth. Jax swipes at his own mouth to clue Billy in.

"Out." Billy wipes the wrong side of his mouth.

"You made a deal. I kept my end!" On my way to the bus this morning, I ran by Billy's house to make sure Mr. Milke's potion worked. Billy's roses are the best on the block.

Billy groans to Jax. "Dude, can you tell her to chill?"

"No can do." Jax looks at me and grins. "Even if I wanted."

Billy scoops up his taco. "Fine. I'm in. But I have detention, so I'll meet you there." He crunches another bite from his table taco.

Did I hold Billy to his word? My shoulders straighten.

Jax nudges Billy. "See, that wasn't so bad, was it, *Fifty-Three?*"

My eyes bulge. *Uh-oh,* the nickname I gave Billy because of his fifty-three freckles.

Billy grits his teeth like he wants to strangle Jax. "Don't ever call me that, *Juniper.*"

Jax pushes his lunch tray aside. "So, we're going there, huh?"

"Stop it, you two!" I point at Billy. "From now on, you're Billy!" I whip my finger at Jax. "And you're Jax. Got it?"

"Fine." Billy shoves the rest of his taco in his mouth.

"But she's still Dandy," Jax whispers.

Billy snorts, and the two of them slap hands. I'm not sure I'll ever understand boys.

"Here's the plan," I say and lean in to get their attention. "All we have to do—"

Our table suddenly fills with noisy kids.

"What?" Jax yells.

"Can't hear you!" Billy chimes in.

"Tell you later!" I scream, barely hearing myself over the noise.

The whole table stops and stares at me. I close my mouth, and Billy opens his—to show me his chewed food. *Holy Monkeys, that's gross!*

I force my gaze away, but my mind still sees globs of cheese mashed with brown meat and chunks of taco shell. My cheeks puff out, and my stomach swirls.

Billy starts to laugh and half-chokes on his mouthful.

Good. I squeeze my lids shut and wait for the heave. Nothing happens, and I realize I don't need to throw up. I'm getting better at holding back, probably because Billy being disgusting is the norm. But my appetite for peanut butter or anything mushed disappears. I fold my sandwich in a napkin, whispering my goodbyes, and give it a proper sandwich burial.

When the bell rings, Billy stands and grabs my half-eaten apple, crunches a bite, and takes it with him.

After school, Jax hands Mr. Jennings a note to get off at my stop.

"Everything looks in order." Mr. Jennings tucks the note in his shirt pocket. "Grab a seat."

Once we sit, I explain to Jax that I think this whole jinx thing is not just about Mr. Dally. "We need to help Billy, too."

"That's what I was trying to tell you," Jax says.

Mr. Milke tried to tell me, too. Now I get it; Billy must believe in the possible to do the impossible.

The bus drops us off, and we take our time getting to Mr.

Dally's, unsure how long Billy will have detention.

"Wait up!" Billy yells from the corner of Mr. Dally's street. He sprints over to us.

My eyes widen. "How did you get done so soon?"

"I swear, you're such a newb. Teachers act like they'll keep you forever, but they wanna get home, too."

"Billy's the expert." Jax bumps his knuckle. "But don't try it. They might keep you."

"Or they'd give her ice cream." Billy pretends like he's scooping ice cream onto a cone. "Here you go, Sweety Pumpkin." He bats his lashes and fake hands it to me.

I push his empty hand away. "No, they wouldn't."

"I'm just saying—" Billy's eyes trail toward the Dally's house. He jumps off the curb and races across the road.

Jax and I look at each other and laugh.

"What's so funny?" Billy shouts from the other side.

Jax shouts, "We're not even in front of the house. Come back over."

Billy mumbles something and creeps back like a skittish cat. When he steps on the curb close to us, Jax shouts, "Boo!"

Billy punches Jax in the arm. "Dude, I'm going to kick your b—"

Jax jumps up and down, laughing and making his arm dangle. "Dead arm, dead arm."

"Forget you guys." Billy shoves his hands in his pants pockets and stomps away. "You wanna risk your life, that's on you. I'm out."

"Wait. Billy, you promised!" I run up to him—Jax follows.

Billy keeps walking. "Not happening."

"We have to," I say. "Mr. Dally's stuck inside and lonely. Plus, we owe him. Remember how he gave everyone vegetables?"

Billy wrinkles his nose. "I don't even like vegetables. Besides, it's not like anything I'd do would help."

"It would too!" Jax says.

"Stay," I plead. "We can't do it by ourselves. We need you."

Billy's face dulls. He slows down and stares at the sidewalk.

"Dude, you can't go back on your promise," Jax reminds him.

Billy pauses and peers between Jax and me, fiddling with his jacket sleeve. "Fine." He sighs. "One try. Got it?"

My neck hurts from nodding too hard. The three of us walk up to the edge of the sidewalk in front of the Dally's.

Billy gives us one last desperate stare. "You sure?"

I wave him on. "You can do it."

He shakes out his hands and cracks his neck. Billy does an about-face and peers over his shoulder, then sprints backward across the sidewalk and says, "Me not, me not, me not." Once he makes it to the other side, he jerks his head up at the same dreary house, and his face falls. "I told you. Nothing happened. You guys don't know what you're talking about. I'm going home."

"Wait, Billy, look." I point to the edge of the grass. "Something did happen. This patch wasn't green before."

Billy squints at the brown lawn from the other side. "I see a little green."

"Me too." Jax waves him back over to our side.

Billy zigs out to the road, avoiding the sidewalk, and zags back to us. "Now, what?"

"I don't know," I say. But I know it's not Billy's fault. Too much sad smog surrounds the house. I'm stuck—my brain freezes, and there goes the plan. Just like the journal—shred to pieces.

But Dr. Richter says if a plan doesn't work, then try another option. I already used Mr. Milke's potion, so I stare at the house, not coming up with anything.

I wish Mr. Milke were here. He would know what to do.

As I'm trying to decide how to tell Jax our plan's doomed, the last autumn leaf falls from the withering oak tree and glides toward us in a spin. I glance up and see Floss peering over the branches. He scuttles away before I can cheer. The leaf sways back and forth, falling to the ground, and lands beside my sneaker. I pick it up. Written across the leaf, in the tiniest print, is a note.

Dearest Miss Dandy,
Trust yourself. You know what to do. You always have.
Respectfully, Mr. Milke

Billy peeks over my shoulder. "Why are you staring at a leaf?" He can't see the writing.

Jax wiggles his brow at me. He can.

Trust myself? But I didn't even know what to do in the first place. Or . . . Maybe I do.

It's still Billy. He needs to know that believing in our plan will make all the difference. He must decide on our next step. I jerk my head toward Billy so Jax can see. Fingers crossed he gets the message. "Okay guys, any ideas? Any at all."

"I'm out of ideas." Jax lifts his shoulders. "How about you, Billy?"

Aw, Jax really does get me.

Billy sits on the curb like he's thinking. I can almost see a cartoon thought bubble with question marks and exclamation points hanging over his head. I try not to laugh. Jax doesn't make it easier when he side-eyes me and grimaces.

Jax pulls out a blade of grass and sticks it in between his teeth. My teeth ache while I wait for Billy to come up with something. I know what I want him to say, but he needs to work it out on his own.

Billy finally speaks. "Well, didn't Mr. Dally like flowers and stuff, like before the jinx? We could maybe plant some?"

"Right! And where do we get flowers?" I sound like Mr. Milke with Floss. I wonder if it feels this good when he helps Floss figure stuff out.

Jax winks, catching where I'm going.

Billy perks up. "We can get some from your dad's shop."

"We cooould." I try to come up with an excuse without lying or revealing my idea. "But we. Ummm—"

"Don't have any money," Jax says.

"Right." Billy scratches his head. "How about we get some flowers from my house?" He doesn't sound confident.

"We totally can." Jax cheers and takes off like Billy's idea exploded out of him. He races down the street.

"What's his deal?" Billy asks. "We're gonna have to move to keep up with him."

"His deal?" I take off and pump my arms to keep pace with Billy. "Flowers are the answer," I say between breaths. But I can't tell him why. The potion made the flowers grow, which means there might be a little magic left in the stems.

We struggle to catch Jax. He finally slows down in front of Billy's house. I gulp air.

Billy slides behind a light post, tipping his head to the side to peek at his house. "It's so strange. You said you'd plant flowers, but *woah*." His patio is in full bloom with lots of flowers in colors I've never seen before.

"So weird." I smile and give Jax a brow wiggle.

Jax smirks back at me. "Weirdest thing I've ever seen."

The three of us approach the grass, and Billy digs in his heels. "I changed my mind. We should go to one of your houses instead."

"Billy, it's fine." I know why he's nervous. "We don't have to go inside. We grab a flower or two, at the roots—so we get the whole plant—and that's it."

"I don't know." Billy eyes his front door.

"It's okay. We'll be quick." I give the wave signal, and we descend upon the lawn from different directions. It's like we're deep in the jungle on a secret military mission. We creep to the patio on our hands and knees. I give them the okay sign when we hit the front patio and tug gently on a rose bush near the root. It slides from the mulch with the root intact. I hold the flower for the guys to see.

Jax holds up a marigold with a grin, while Billy manages to cut a violet in half.

I throw up my hands.

"At the roots," I whisper loud as I can. "Take it gently by the roots." We need to replant the whole memory with every bit of magic the flower contains.

Billy nods and pulls another violet out, intact. I give him a thumbs-up and point down the street. "Go!"

Halfway across the lawn, the sprinklers start to spray. "Dang it!" Billy yells.

The front door creaks, and Mr. Simpson yells, "Billy? You better get your butt inside!"

We don't stop until we hit the corner.

Jax asks Billy, "You gonna be in trouble?"

"Yeah, just like every day."

I glance back at Billy's house and wonder if there are enough flowers in the world to help Mr. Simpson.

Billy shakes water droplets from his hair, and the three of us laugh. We're all soaked, and my clothes stick to me a little, but we're still smiling, so I don't mind. We check over our haul. Billy's violet looks the best, and Jax's marigold looks the worst, but they're all going to work; I know it.

"Well, I better head back." Billy hands me his violet. "You two can take it from here."

Jax asks, "Are you sure you don't want to go with us?"

Billy hesitates, picking at a scab on his elbow. "No, dude. If I don't go now, it'll be way worse."

"I get it." Jax bumps elbows with Billy. "Thanks for the help."

Billy tilts his chin up at me and heads back toward his house.

"He's not so bad, I guess," I say.

"Yeah. He's a good dude."

I watch Billy walk away and decide he and I will always be friends—maybe not the same close we once were, or as close as Jax and me—but we're on the same team.

23

GINGER COOKIES AND TEA

"What now?" Jax asks.

The *Farmers' Almanac* fills in my head. I didn't just read it for fun. It's Dad's favorite website and sometimes mine. It predicts all kinds of things, like the best planting days and meteor showers, although a meteor shower won't help us right now.

"So, I've been thinking. Billy started to reverse the jinx, but it needs a little more work," I tell him. "And who cares what Floggy says." I suspect Floss is Floggy, anyway. "We can do this ourselves. We just need to figure out how." My shoulders straighten, and my mind feels sharp and confident like I can conquer this. "Remember that one night at my house? You said we would have a cool adventure?"

Jax breaks into a sly smile. "I remember."

"Let's have one." I organize the flowers gently in the backpacks.

The next moment, my mind explodes with options to help Mr. Dally. It's like a puzzle. Each idea leads to another. Jax crosses and uncrosses his arms like he's thinking, while I . . . *I got it!*

"We're in fifth grade, so for luck, we need five moves to save Mr. Dally." I jump over a puddle. "Follow me."

"Where're we going?" he asks as we race down the street.

Taking a right, then left, we stop at McNally's corner store. I push the glass door and jump through the entry. "Step one. We need ginger cookies. And sweet tea. Oh, and chocolate."

Jax scratches his head. "For what?"

"To trade. Grams' tea ladies love ginger cookies. We need tea for mulch. And everyone likes chocolate."

We breeze down the aisles until I spot the cookies Grams swears belong on this side of heaven and grab a box. I head to the refrigerator and grab a can of sweet tea. At the checkout, I pick out a chocolate bar with caramel from the rack. "These, please." I place the items on the counter, and the man barely pays us attention while he rings us up.

I rummage through my backpack for spare change to pay him and stuff the cookies, tea, and chocolate into the pack.

"Okay. Step two. Find a spider plant. It has long blades." I spread my hands apart to show Jax how long. "And pointed tips that kind of looks like grass, but grows best in the shade, or a pot. It could also hang from one of those bowl planters."

"And we need a spider plant, why?"

"For Ms. Bittle's cat."

He scratches his head. "That makes sense."

"I know, right?" I take off through the parking lot. Jax doesn't take long to catch up.

"Car!" I yell and point to a blue Volkswagen. We freeze,

pretending to be trees. My toes dig into the sneakers, and I struggle to keep balance. Once it drives past, we cut through a lawn.

"Truck!" Jax screams and hits the grass. I nosedive beside him. The truck speeds past, and he lifts his head. "New rule. If it's a truck, we take cover. If there isn't any grass, we duck."

I acknowledge his rule with a nod and jump to my feet.

We stay on the lookout for a spider plant, moving from house to house and creeping up lawns. Finally, Jax points to a hanging pot.

"That's rosemary." Then I remember Dad delivered plants to Mr. Jennings last week. I'm pretty sure one was a spider.

"Mr. Jennings' house," I say.

"Do you know where he lives?"

I point south.

A block over, we hunch down behind thick bushes fencing off his house. I peek through the mass of twisted branches and cross my fingers, scouting the front door. "There! On the front porch."

We sneak across the lawn and drop to our bellies, skootching through the fallen leaves and moving closer to accomplishing our mission. Once we reach the spider plant, I carefully pull a small handful of the blade-like leaves, keeping the roots attached. "This should do." I place them in the backpack and leave the chocolate on the doormat. "Payment."

Minutes later, we cut through the alley and into the park, where the groundskeeper is trimming the plants. "Step three. We need mulch to plant the flowers. Not too much. Three handfuls should do from that fertilizer bag over there. Put it in here." I hand Jax my empty lunch bag.

While Jax gets the potting soil, I sneak my hand through the bush to set the sweet tea beside the groundskeeper's feet.

"Got it," Jax says.

"Good job." I tuck the bag back into my backpack, and we take off out of the park, then down the road two blocks.

The next step in our plan: Ms. Bittle's house.

Her tabby cat is perched on the windowsill, sprawled out soaking up the sun. Misty regards us coolly. I guess the cat senses we aren't a threat because he yawns, hunches his back in a stretch, and jumps to the porch. Then I spot the jasmine plant hanging in the front window inside the house.

"We have to get some of those flowers." I point to the plant.

"Because the cat needs it?"

"Of course not. Misty wants the spider plant. It's like cat salad. *We* need the jasmine. It helps ward off bad energy."

Jax gives me a funny stare. "How do you know all this stuff?"

"Facts. I'm good at facts. And math. Probably those two things. And because of the perks, you know? My dad having a plant shop. With tea."

Jax seems impressed, and until now, I hadn't realized how much I knew. My head buzzes with excitement. "Let's go."

We sprint up the drive and onto the porch. The tabby weaves in and out between our shins, keeping his nose on my backpack. I ring the doorbell and pull the cookies from the pack.

Ms. Bittle peeks out her peephole and opens the door with a curious smile. "Meredith, how nice to see you." Today, she's wearing a blue robe. Her hair's still in curlers.

"Hello, Ms. Bittle. I've brought a friend." My chest feels

like exploding when I say, *friend*. "His name's Jax, and we came to make you some tea."

"Tea?" Her smile beams. "Well, come in."

The house is colder than a winter's day, as Grams would say. I wrap my arms around myself to ward off the shivers. Knitted scarves and kitten fabric quilts covered in orange and black cat hairs are spread out all over the room. I hold back a sneeze and pull out my teabags. "Dad and I made a fresh batch of rosehip."

"Wonderful. Have a seat." She motions us to sit at the kitchen table, and I scoot stacks of white doilies to the side to make room for the cookies. Ms. Bittle prepares the kettle on the stove.

"You drink fruit tea, young man?"

"Um. No. But I make my mom tea all the time. Maybe I can help?"

"That's okay. How about a nice glass of chocolate milk?"

"Sure!"

My leg won't stop jittering, but I do my best not to rush her. We need to make time for Ms. Bittle. Mr. Dally would understand, with her being alone too.

Ms. Bittle spends the next thirty minutes talking about how she decided to name her cat Misty, even though he's a boy, but she swears he loves the name. I'm not sure. Misty side-eyes her when she gushes about how he answered to it right away. He does get a bit friendlier when I pull out the spider plant.

"I also brought you this. It's a spider plant, and it's not harmful to cats. Like a *salad*. But they really shouldn't eat much; just if they do, it's safe." Misty wrinkles his nose at the word salad. "You can plant the roots, and it will grow." I glance at the window. "I bet the spider will look nice next to your jasmine."

"Oh, the jasmine." Ms. Bittle glances at the window plant. "I remember. You sold me that beauty this summer."

"It's really pretty." I squeeze my fist tight to get courage. It's rude to ask for things. But is it impolite if I'm asking for a friend? I take the plunge. "Do you mind if I take a few petals, Ms. Bittle? For a friend."

"Take as much as you like, dear."

Jax nudges me, and I grin. Score four!

I thank Ms. Bittle and clip two flowers gently with my fingernails, placing them carefully in the empty lunch bag.

We wave goodbye, and she shuts the door.

Jax smiles. "She's real nice."

"I know. She's lonely. My dad says the best gift you can give a person is your time. 'A hot cup of tea and twenty minutes of conversation works wonders.' Doesn't seem like a lot of time, but it is to them."

"So, what's with the jasmine?"

"You'll see." I take off, and he follows, one block over, then another, and we take a right.

190

We stand in front of the sidewalk staring at the Dally's, my lungs out of breath. Once the jinx breaks, I hope that no one ever calls the house anything but the Dally's ever again.

Jax inspects the curtains drawn in the front window. "The place is still doomed, right?"

"Yes." A haze of smog hovers over the house and covers the front yard. No matter which way we go, we're jinxed.

But we must stop the smog from spreading before it gets worse. I remember when the cloud formed—the day Mrs. Dally died. I watched as its pollution thickened day after day until it covered the house. A mixture of sadness and loneliness rolled into this dark cloud and sucked out all of Mr. Dally's happiness. It's been coming for me, too. I could sense it before I met Jax again.

"Can we get past the lawn?" Jax asks.

"There must be a way." I calculate all possible paths. Step five is the big one.

Got it. I drop the backpack to the sidewalk, take out the flowers we collected at Billy's, and line them next to one of the cracks.

"We can do this," I assure Jax, "but we have to do it together."

He rolls out his shoulders. "Okay, ready."

"First, we need to sneeze to get rid of the bad pollution," I tell him. "Next, we close our eyes. We think good thoughts. Since we want to help Mr. Dally, we need to think of things that used to make him happy, like his garden, and Halloween, and Mrs. Dally. Pick two for good luck, and we'll take turns saying them out loud."

Jax's brows furrow like he's thinking. "Okay. I've got two,

191

but what if I don't have to sneeze?"

"You will." I smile to give him confidence. "But if you can't, do your best."

Together, we take our first step inside the sidewalk square.

Ah-choo, I sneeze. "Zucchinis and Mrs. Dally's iced tea." I dip my left eye into my shoulder to be careful, but I refuse to say, "Not me, not me, not me." I can hear my heartbeat, and the cadence sort of sounds like *not me, not me, not me.* Super-fast. Which is not cheating. I can't force my heart not to protect itself.

The dust swirls and rumbles, creeping back from the middle of the lawn.

We take the second step.

Ah-choo. Jax's fake sneeze makes him real sneeze. *Ah-choo.* He scrunches his nose and raises his voice. "First place at the Harvest Fest and Mrs. Dally's smile!"

A funnel of smog rises to the rooftop and hovers.

I'm about to panic that we haven't sneezed enough, when I spot Floss on a tree branch, his cheeks puffed out, and he's blowing at the dense fog. The wind gusts, sweeping autumn leaves into the billowing soot cloud.

"Come on. You can do it, Floss!" I call out.

Jax spots him and cheers. "You can do it, Floss!"

The cloud rises a few feet, then sinks like it doesn't have enough power.

"It's not enough!" I tell Jax. "We have to help him. Quick, get my bag. Grab the jasmine."

"Walk backward?"

"No," I tell him. "Together. Two hops back."

We hop backward, and he leans back to reach into the bag,

then hands me the jasmine. I take the flower petals and roll them into a tight wad on my jeans. The jasmine's too mangled. This isn't going to work. Then I remember Billy's paper footballs. "In the side backpack pocket. Grab those paper strips."

Jax unzips the pockets, rummages around, and hands me the unfolded footballs. I wad the paper tightly with the jasmine. It's tiny but not as small as the ball at Mr. Milke's amusement park. If I could put that between two clown teeth, I can do this.

Judging by the wind speed, it's going to be close. I wind up, snap my hand back, and toss the ball straight in the air. It barely travels, like I threw a paper ball. Which I did.

Step five—*failure.*

My head drops, like my neck turned to mush. I thought it would work.

"It's okay," he says. "We'll come up with something else."

Jax penguin-nudges me, and warmth spreads through my arm, making its way to my heart.

Now I know he's my real friend. He accepts me, no matter what.

A gush of air suddenly catches the ball, lifting it higher and higher. The paper and jasmine join the funnel, spinning and twisting, mixing with dust and pollen particles. The whirlwind sucks all the particles into the sky like a tornado vacuum and disappears.

"Hurry. Let's go!" I yank Jax's hand.

We bolt across the sidewalk like it's no big deal. Or Jax does. My heart almost explodes.

"We did it!" I yell once we're on the other side.

Jax high-fives me.

I run back to the backpack and take out a pack of zucchini seeds. I grab my journal and a pen. Crossing the dead grass, I kneel and sprinkle the seeds where the old garden used to be.

Then, I sit on the curb and write in the journal.

Dear Mr. Dally,

I'm sorry I didn't come and visit. I don't want to forget anyone anymore. I miss Mrs. Dally, too, and I want to be your friend again. Here is a journal of things I learned about friendship, in case you forgot how.

Yours truly,

Meredith

p.s. If you give Jax a chance, I think you might like him, too. I'm glad I did.

I place the journal on the front step. "You're fine now, Mr. Dally."

Jax joins me. We dig the holes and plant the flowers beneath the front window. When we finish, I glance up at the windows and hope Mr. Dally can see us.

24

FOXES DANCE THE JITTERBUG

Pumpkin and corn stalks decorate the neighborhood—tiny curls of ash from a chimney float in the thick air. October means fireplaces and sweaters. I've decided fall is my favorite season.

Jax puts his thumb up and measures the afternoon sun. "Here, next to the porch steps, has the right amount of shade." He digs the hole.

I hand him a violet and measure the distance to the next flower.

Jax and I replanted Mr. Dally's garden, using flower bulbs from Billy's and vegetables from Dad's shop. It's like a whole new house. But to be safe, we never pull flowers from the same spot at the Simpson's. Billy still needs some magic.

The first day we planted, nothing happened. Yesterday, I caught Mr. Dally watching us from his second-floor window. Today is day three.

The front door creaks open. Jax and I look up, and I catch my breath. Mr. Dally's grey fedora hat tips out, and then I see his white hair. He tilts his nose up and sniffs the air, which is the best news. Today smells like a happy kind of day.

Tap. Tap. Tap. A metal cane steadies his step. He stops and takes a breath, and then another step. Four steps later, he crosses the yard to us. "That's a lovely flower bed you've planted." He braces his lower back with one hand and reaches down to touch a petal with the other. "Do you know the violet is a sister of the pansy? My wife, Beth, loved pansies."

"I know where I can get some." Jax rubs his nose and leaves a smudge of dirt. "I'll bring a few."

Mr. Dally claps him on the back. "Thank you. Both of you."

I slide a chair from the door beside us, and Mr. Dally sits. For the next hour, he tells us about the benefits of each type of flower. "Now, the sweet violet, it works miracles on inflammation. Which is great for these old hips."

I lean against the tree and soak in his words. I missed his voice even more than I remembered.

When Mr. Dally finally stands, he says, "Well, I better get ready. I have an appointment in a little while."

"We'll come back tomorrow," I assure him.

"I'll look forward to that." Mr. Dally shuts his front door.

"Holy Monkeys. Can you believe it? We did it. Mr. Dally's going to be fine."

"Best news ever." Jax slides a blade of grass between his teeth.

"Okay, time's up," I tell him, packing the gardening tools. "You better go get ready. It's about time for my birthday party."

I've held in the excitement all day.

Today, I'm eleven!

Last night, I had a dream my parents threw a huge birthday

party at my house. Except it wasn't my real house, and we rode on unicorns. There was even a skulk of foxes, which taught us how to dance the jitterbug. Mr. Milke wasn't at the party, so it was a regular dream. No way he'd miss the jitterbug.

I'm not having a party like the one in my dream, but Jax is coming over. I sent an invitation to Mr. Milke and Floss, too.

When I get home, Dad sends me upstairs to clean my room. Every year he does the same thing so that I can come down the stairs, and he can yell, "Happy Birthday." He always holds a special homemade cake with the trick candles that never blow out. I play along because he loves it.

Mom and I went clothes shopping last week, and she made a big fuss about what I should wear on my birthday. I picked out a sweatshirt with kittens. They're holding up their paws. She asked if I was sure I wanted to wear a kitten shirt for my birthday. Of course, I did. It says, *It's my Paw-ty.*

I pounce on the bed and pull out a new journal from the side table. This one has *Farmers' Almanac* written on the front with vegetables—a zucchini seed packet marks my spot. I slide my finger down to open the last written page.

Dear Diary,

Today, Jax and I planted violets at the Dally's. And Mr. Dally finally came out! He even stayed with us and mentioned Mrs. Dally. That's good. I don't ever want him to forget her.

Oh, and Jax and I are now good as new friends. And Billy, too, in our own way.

And guess what? Today I'm eleven! Can you believe it?

Sincerely,

Meredith Denise Smart. (Dandy)

I tuck the journal back in the drawer and peek out the window. No one is coming up the walkway. Hopefully, Jax's already here. Now, all I have to do is pretend I'm surprised.

"Meredith, can you come here, please?" Dad shouts a few minutes later.

My feet clump down the stairs one step at a time, and I plaster a smile on my face.

As I get halfway down, Mom jumps out, holding a cake. "Surprise!" she yells, wearing Dad's chef hat, which *does* surprise me since I was expecting Dad.

Jingles barks and jumps around the room. His tail wags at people popping out from places I didn't think would make clever spots to hide. Grams stands behind a chair, and Isabel and Alexa jump out from behind the couch. Who invited them? Even Molly peeks from behind the living room curtains. She's wearing a kitten shirt, too!

Mr. Dally is standing in the corner, talking to Ms. Bittle and offering Misty a treat. The finicky cat paws the snack, twisting away from her grip. Jingles watches the tabby but keeps his distance. Smart, if you ask me. Ms. Bittle's even wearing a dress, and her hair is fluffed out.

Weird. She looks like Misty.

Billy's here too, leaning against a wall by himself. He didn't jump out from anywhere. I don't think Billy's the surprise kind of guy. He's staring at Molly, and his face is mushy as fresh biscuit dough, almost like he's in a daze. What's that all about?

Which reminds me, where's Jax? I can't see him anywhere. My heart starts to worry, and my knobby knees shake. I suck the nervous back down. There's no way Jax won't show. Is there? No, he'll show.

My toes curl as I clunk down the remaining steps and hum to drown out the noise. My cheeks are sore, but I keep smiling because I'm supposed to. I thank everyone for coming, and Dad proclaims, "Food is served!"

Everyone cheers and follows him into the kitchen. He passes by Mom and stops to kiss her cheek—my heart double skips when Mom gives him that gooey gaze and brushes her hand down his arm.

Dad's filled every counter with his best inventions, like peanut butter pancakes and chicken nuggets coated in salty pretzel bits. There is a big bottle of Heinz ketchup—and a bowl with packets for me.

Pop-crack-spark.

Floss perches on the countertop and watches Grams' milkshake blender whip round and round.

Good. He got the invitation. Jingles spots Floss and takes off, racing around the kitchen island, barking up at him. Floss blows him a raspberry.

Grams stands on her stool, surrounded by all kinds of ice cream and bowls filled with candy and fruits, even sprinkles. Billy orders a strawberry shake with sour candy.

Don't gag. Don't gag.

Brrrr. The blender whirls. I'm about to warn Floss about the risks of blender-watching when his big eyes roll back and he crashes to the floor. *Kssch!*

Jingles stops and jerks his head at me like he expects me to help the trickster beetle.

Floss hangs his head and staggers under the counter to hide. I cover my hand over my mouth and try not to laugh.

"For my special birthday girl." Grams hands me a vanilla shake. "I can't believe you're eleven. Feels like only yesterday, you were a curious toddler."

The doorbell rings.

"Meredith, can you get the door?" Mom asks, passing out bags of popcorn mixed with M&M's and raisins.

I count the number of people here while I walk to the door. *Fifteen!* My house shouldn't have this many people inside. Buildings have occupancy codes and stuff. I bet homes have them.

Mrs. Cooper yells, "Happy Birthday!" when I open the door, and Jax gives me a half-smile.

Dad rushes to the door. "May I?" he asks and gestures at her wheelchair.

"Thank you." Mrs. Cooper rests her hands in her lap.

Dad takes the handles of Mrs. Cooper's chair and lifts the front wheels over the bottom of the door frame, then the rear ones. "Wait until you see what's on the menu, Dalila. Oh, and we're serving honeysuckle tea."

"How lovely." Mrs. Cooper smiles her wide, pretty smile. I fight the urge to warn her about Floss.

Jax waits until they're in the kitchen before he speaks to me. "Sorry I'm late. Mom had a rough day."

"Is she okay?"

"Yes. I think so."

"I'm glad you both came." I point to a bag of tea on the entry table. "Dad and I made a special batch of chamomile tea for your mom to take home. It's good for her. Chamomile helps to relax."

"She'll like that." Jax's eyes mist a bit. "How about you? You okay?"

"It's nice," I say. "Very nice. Thank you for coming." I hold back a scream.

He watches me. "You sure you're okay?"

I can't hold it in any longer. "No. This isn't good. What if there's a fire?" I twist my hands together. "It's too loud. There are too many people here, and I bet it's against fire department code. I'm going to get arrested at my party!"

"Guess we'll move the party to the jailhouse." He wiggles a brow.

"What? No," I whisper.

"I'm kidding." Jax grimaces. "We won't get arrested. You're nervous. If you need to, close your eyes for a minute to get a break from seeing everyone. Count down from thirty. It's a trick my dad taught me. Give it a try."

"Okay." I take a deep breath and try. ". . . four, three, two, one."

"How do you feel?" he asks, brows raised.

"Just Dandy."

Billy snorts from the other side of the room. "Ha! Funny."

Jax grins and then gets serious. "Listen. I know this isn't your kind of thing, but Grams gave me strict orders not to tell you anyone else might come."

"She's kind of scary." Billy leans against the wall and slurps from the strawberry milkshake Grams made for him.

"It's okay," I tell Jax. "She really wanted a party."

Mom yells to us from the kitchen, "Get your food before it's all gone."

"Coming," I say and turn back to Jax. "Everything should be done in about an hour or so. Stay after."

At the end of the party, I see everyone off.

"Thank you for coming," I repeat for the eighth time. Isabel hands me an envelope and hugs me at the door. I stand with arms glued to my sides like a cardboard statue and wiggle my fingers to stop the numb tingling. I count the colors in her hairband, which is twelve, and she finally lets go.

"Fun party, Meredith. Thanks for the invite." Isabel smiles at me while Alexa gazes at Jax.

"See you at school on Monday?" Alexa asks Jax.

"Yep. *We'll* see you Monday," he answers.

Alexa tugs on Isabel's arm. "Let's go."

"Here, let me get the door," Billy offers with a sly smirk. "Off you go, ladies."

Isabel steps outside, and Alexa follows. When Alexa hits the front step—

Fllleeep! Billy farts extra loud.

"Alexa!" he yells, waving his hand in front of his nose. "Disgusting."

"I didn't." Her mouth shoots wide open. "You did that!"

"See you Monday." Billy shuts the door. Jax gives him a low-five.

"That wasn't nice," I say, but secretly I think it was kinda funny.

"Yeah. Well, nice doesn't always work." Billy punches Jax on the shoulder. "I'm out of here. See you two losers later." Stepping out the front door, he shoves his hands in his pants pockets and struts down the walk. Jax shuts the door.

"Well?" He gestures at Isabel's pink envelope in my hand.

I open it. Inside is an invitation to her party next month. There are stickers, and right over the "I" in Isabel's name is a heart.

"I got one, too." Jax waves his card.

Last year, all I wanted was stickers and a heart. Today, I tuck the invitation in my pocket.

Only adults are left, so my parents take over the goodbyes. I hear Dad offer Mr. Dally a job at the flower shop on his way out.

Jax and I escape to the backyard. I grab the middle swing seat. My best friend sits beside me. We take turns jumping off to see who can land the farthest. I win. I'm pretty sure Jax let me.

Mr. Milke joins us and sits on Jax's shoulder. I wasn't sure he would come. He's been trilling around the party the last half-hour or so. Only Jax and I noticed. I'm glad he showed. I haven't seen much of Mr. Milke or even Floss now that Jax and I have each other. We're too busy hanging out. I don't forget them, or any of my friends at the *Dandy-lion*, but I'm all right. Mr. Milke knew best: I was in charge all along, and all I needed was to trust myself.

"Happy birthday, Miss Dandy." Mr. Milke flutters over and tips his top hat.

Grams brings us out fresh milkshakes. Jax takes his shake from the tray, mint chocolate chips with Gummi Bears. Grams must have rubbed off on him. I try not to gag when he sucks green chunky bear heads through his straw. She hands me vanilla.

Mr. Milke whizzes around Jax's shake.

"You'll have to wait for yours." Grams looks directly at him before heading back inside.

Jax and I stare at each other and then at Mr. Milke.

"Did Grams just talk to *you?*" I ask.

Mr. Milke winks and flies off. For some reason, that makes sense.

"Doesn't surprise me a bit." Jax hops off the swing and rummages through the flowers nearby.

I'm about to ask him what he's doing when Dad joins us out back and gives me a big hug, the soft, squishy kind that makes me feel special. "Did you have a great party?"

"The best," I say and mean it. Today was perfect—for real.

"How's my mom?" Jax asks.

"She's fine. You two hang out. She's having tea in the kitchen with us."

Jax nods. He has the same face Jingles gets when he takes something he's not supposed to, his hands tucked behind his back.

"What do you have there?" Dad asks, eyeing him. Jax's cheeks turn deep red, which is weird because he's never embarrassed.

"Something I got for Da—Meredith."

"Well, let's see it then." Dad's brow quirks.

Jax pulls a clay flowerpot out from behind his back that's been hand-painted. There's a tuxedo-wearing hummingbird dancing with a daffodil—two stick people pose like trees beside them. I'm the one with the fluffy hair, or I hope I am since the other one looks like Jax.

"For me?" Inside the pot is a dandelion.

"What a perfect gift," Dad says. "Let's get your plant inside and give it food, shall we?"

"Be right back," I tell Jax and take the pot. Once Jax is out of earshot, I whisper, "He got me a weed."

Dad smiles and kneels next to me. "People often give bad names to beautiful things. Do you see the puffs sprouting from the middle?"

I nod.

"They're seeds. The puff part is like a parachute, carrying the seed to where it needs to be. The dandelion is a wise plant and knows precisely what it needs to do."

Like me.

"Be gentle with it. Dandelions are sensitive. Even the slightest touch or the smallest breeze makes the seeds blow away."

I glimpse back at Jax. He gives me a thumbs-up, and everything finally makes sense, why they call me Dandy. Dandelions are sensitive, too.

Taking a deep breath, I blow on the instinctive flower, scattering the parachute seeds across the grass.

"Or you can do that." Dad laughs, and I curtsy.

My world feels right.

That's the thing about dandelions. We get carried away. It's what we're meant to do.

ACKNOWLEDGEMENTS

Unlike chapters, my thanks come in no specific order. Without each, this would be no book.

These pages accumulated under the guidance of the most patient teachers: fellow authors. My attempts to put pen to paper would have been tragic if it were not for writing groups—shout-out to the Central Phoenix Writing Group and Armadillo Authors. I am lucky to be associated with these talented writers.

To my stellar crew of critique partners, teachers, beta's, and editors who helped form my style, Brian Jesse, Jacob Shaver, Matthew Howard, Jeff Duntemann, Steven Catling, and the mighty Four4ce. Dani Camarena, Leah Downing, and Jill Richards. Together we climb.

Getting published is both hard work and a hefty sprinkle of luck. My chance of success would have been rubbish if not for WriteMentor, and my mentor Caroline Murphy choosing the Curious World of Dandy-lion for the showcase.

To my young beta readers, who shaped Meredith and Jax's world in so many magical ways. Abby Rasmussen, Anastasia Sanchez, Scarlet Richards, and Harmony Mosier, you make writing worthwhile.

To the team at Lawley Publishing. Wow. Thank you for picking me. I am so grateful.

And what about those illustrations! I am so over-the-moon thrilled to have been paired with the talented Jocie Salveson.

Chris, my husband, I am grateful for the calm you bring to my life—not to mention the best home-cooked meals. You have always encouraged my goals and dreams, no matter how high.

To my daughter, Sam, and son-in-law, Brendan, for never wavering in your belief this book would see print. You emboldened me to put myself out there, enter the contest, and send out queries. I'll never forget the days spent discussing my characters as if they were real. Of course, they were.

And to my family. The in-laws, the out-laws, blood and married-to, friends forged into family, and a very special mentee. For never doubting that I would give it a shot, you made it easier for me to believe in myself.

I am forever humbled to have all of you in my life.

Lorraine Hawley lives in Gilbert, Arizona, and writes stories about tweens, teens, and fantastical worlds. While she has attempted to write non-magical stories, her characters have refused to stay reality grounded, leaping off the pages to fly. So she gave up trying to be what she is not, accepting her role of a fantasy writer who hopes to share magic with the world.

Lorraine enjoys connecting with others in literature and is enthusiastic about sharing writing tips. Drop by to say hello at **www.lorrainehawley.com** for upcoming events, releases, and other musings of an untethered mind.

Jocie Salveson is a permanently enrolled student of Planet Earth. Born and raised at almost the very center of North America, Jocie gathered her art supplies, eventually moving to Germany, where she traversed glorious mountains for three years in pursuit of knowledge. In her quest, she uncovered a mystical scroll filled with secrets of paintbrush, canvas, and pen. Now residing in Japan, she uses that gift to draw this mostly true tale.

Well-traveled and having lived on three continents with her charming Navy husband and three lovable, adaptable kids, Jocie brings her imagination and at least a set of colored pencils wherever she goes. One can create art anywhere, and that's what she intends to do!

To see her work and discover why she has an affinity for Cyclops, visit **www.jociesalveson.com**.

CPSIA information can be obtained
at www.ICGtesting.com
Printed in the USA
LVHW022213020522
717727LV00006B/656

9 781952 209918